ELSIE WINTERS

A Boundlands Novella

Live, Laugh, Lurk

LIVE, LAUGH, LURK

For information contact: https://www.elsiewinters.com

ASIN: B0DBP562YR

ISBN: 978-1-7375355-6-0

Cover illustration by Amira Naval | navalamira@gmail.com

Editing services provided by Wolffe-Stoirm Publishing

Contents

For Christine and "the Carebears." Thank you for dragging me along in life when I have no strength to drag myself.

Chapter 1

Lilith

I SUPPOSE YOU COULD say the town had a little bit of "Southern Gothic" flair if you were being nice. But if I were completely honest, it kind of gave me the creeps.

I'd never been one for small towns, personally. Elvish people often preferred orderly cities with plenty of amenities, and my family was firmly entrenched in New Caelora. The bustling, busy metropolis of sky rises and one-way streets that made up my home city, the capital of the largest elvish province, enamored me in a way no quirky, empty village ever could. Even downtown Golden Laurel, just a stone's throw from this outer university district I'd moved to, had a couple of gleaming towers made of clean lines of metal and glass, and roving street sweepers that worked nightly to keep the roads pristine. But here? These ramshackle buildings in this little hamlet had never even seen a bucket of soap and water as far as I could tell, let alone a street sweeper. Weeds poked through cracks in the buckled sidewalk. The signs were all faded and peeling to the point of illegibility. Boarded-up windows hid shadowed interiors, and a thick coat of dust and grime covered every surface I could see. If it weren't for the cheerful chatter of college students coming and going, it would have felt like the setting for a ghost story.

I fought a shiver. The encroaching dusk and towering nearby trees probably added to the spooky feeling pervading the street in front of the dated apartment building that was to be my new home, but I also felt a bit... trapped. It had only taken a short search to find a little wyvern-drawn carriage to deliver me from the center of the college town, but out here the streets were vacant. Not a carriage or pull-cart in sight. Getting back *into* town would take more effort.

But this was fine. Really. It would be temporary, regardless of what my uncle thought. I would get the new garden center up and running for him, and then I could go back to managing Blossom and Bonsai—the most profitable, gorgeous nursery in New

Caelora. People like me, who craved a touch of greenery while living in a crowded city, could pop in to peruse the cheerful, leafy offerings and take home a cute little succulent for their desk or a pot of draping vines to grace their windowsill. Just thinking about the adorable, tidy rows of rare and exotic houseplants that made up most of our stock made me wistful—pairing people with the perfect plant match was one of my favorite parts of the job. Since I also had some sylvan ancestry and a bit of plant magic in my veins, I couldn't imagine a more fulfilling career.

At least, until my uncle—who also happened to be my boss—had given me more and more responsibility, to the point that I was managing the nursery for him, and then had the *audacity* to give me puppy eyes when he acquired a new nursery that needed an overhaul out here in the middle of nowhere. Boylen had unfairly effective puppy eyes for an old man. The only reason I'd agreed was because I trusted my younger cousin Melantha to fill my role and keep the shop running in my absence. She'd been learning and growing so much since joining the family business as a teenager, and I knew I could count on our Uncle Boylen to help her if she ran into trouble.

The door banged behind me, and I startled, whirling to find that it was only the pair of college-aged boys whom Boylen had hired to help me move. "It's all in, miss," the biggest one, an orc, said sheepishly, as the much smaller goblin waved goodbye and blinked at me with his overly large eyes. I thanked them both profusely, tipping them extra, and then bid them goodnight. The apartment was already furnished, since I didn't plan on staying permanently, so the move had been easy and relatively swift. But I groaned internally as I watched the young men make their way up the street in the direction of the student housing block, knowing that I still had too much to do before I could sleep tonight—a bed to dress and toiletries to dig out of wherever they were buried in my boxes. I was already making a mental list of groceries I probably wouldn't even be able to find at the rundown little corner market we'd passed on the way in.

The odd sensation of being watched tickled at my periphery, and I hunched my shoulders in response. There was no one else on the quiet block that I could see as I cast my gaze around, looking for the source. It wasn't until I glanced up—several stories up—to the window just above my new third-floor walk-up, that I found two giant, glimmering red eyes reflecting at me out of the shadows. Just perfect. I lived beneath the boogeyman. I didn't even try to fight my full-body shudder.

If I hadn't been listening for it, I probably wouldn't have heard it at all, but the soft click, click, click of my creepy upstairs neighbor pacing around his apartment kept me awake far longer than I was used to. I didn't usually mind hearing my neighbors. I had been living cheek-by-jowl for most of my life, after all. But there was something sinister about the scratching noise, which I could only assume was my upstairs neighbor's claws tapping against the hardwood as he moved about his top floor unit. It reminded me of the sound of rats scurrying in a ceiling and put me on edge the entire night.

The result was a grumpy morning as I stopped by the local coffee shop before heading out to inspect Boylen's new nursery.

The previous owners had really let it go, and since most of the staff had left when they retired, I had a lot of hiring and work to do to return it to its former glory. It wasn't the first time I'd seen it, and I already had some thoughts brewing about how to improve it, but I wanted to talk to the only staffer who'd stayed on—a grouchy old man named Artem, who looked to be at least half dryad. I was used to chatting with my younger cousin any time I needed company at work, or joking around with the guys in the warehouse, so the thought of getting to know a prickly new employee was uncomfortable.

He was tall, with a stalwart build, and smatterings of weathered bark on his skin and tattered leaves growing in his hair marked him as one of the ancient forest warriors. But what stuck out the most about Artem to me was his permanently dour expression. I found he had a hidden soft spot though. "I couldn't leave the plants," he'd muttered grumpily when I asked him why he hadn't left with the others when his former bosses retired. But I decided he was okay. I didn't really mind that he was crotchety as long as he was good at his job. Maybe we could just be crotchety together.

There weren't enough plants in stock to sustain the business, but what we did have was healthy and vibrant, happily thriving under Artem's care. The greenhouse windows were filthy, and weeds grew abundantly between the bricks of the front walk. The first thing I did was hire a stout, gregarious dwarvish man named Jereck to tackle the numerous maintenance needs, the first of which was to paint the front sign. He might have talked entirely too much while he worked, but he was pretty efficient, and within a few hours our new shop—aptly named "The Floral Dilemma"—sported a sign with a pretty cream background and gold letters surrounded by soft green and gold leaves. I was thrilled. The bright, cheerful sign was the first thing that had lifted my mood since I'd arrived in this weird little town. I promptly busied myself with the happy task of placing orders for seeds and succulents, fertilizers and fancy new gardening tools.

My good mood lasted until Artem sidled into my office with a mild sneer on his face.

I realized I'd been humming as I worked. "Sorry, I'll stop humming."

"You can hum," he said gruffly.

"Then what's wrong?" I asked, still on uneven footing with the older gentleman.

He cast a critical eye over my list of orders. "House plants and flowers are all well and good, but we need crop starts and bare root trees for the ones out here who like to grow food."

"Oh." I wilted a little at that. While I had plenty of experience coaching new gardeners through growing cherry tomatoes or dwarf peppers on a balcony garden, my knowledge of fruit trees or larger crop-producing plants was limited. I didn't even have any good suppliers.

"Go up to the university," he said, taking pity on me and gesturing vaguely toward the west. "They've got that horticultural research facility where they breed all kinds of new apples and pears. The last owners were too stubborn to work with them because they didn't like that persnickety head researcher, but he's got some real neat trees up there. They'll even let you try the fruit at one of their tasting events."

So that was how I found myself at a "tasting" one late afternoon, surrounded by baskets of apples and pears and stone fruits all laid out on tables on the edge of an experimental orchard. There were a dozen or so other people milling around, tramping across the mulched gathering area. This was exactly the kind of thing that I would have loved to attend with my friends or my mom back at home, I noted wistfully as I looked around the open space by myself, feeling the loneliness of a new place just a little more intensely.

Several people were moving with purpose to purchase boxes of fruit they'd already pre-ordered, others towing excited children as they marveled at all the different varieties of fruit, so I didn't pay much attention at first when I noticed a small child rampaging around amongst the nearby trees. She was young, with dark hair pulled up in tiny pigtails and light green skin like some of the sylvans and other forest fae. She was squatted down in the dirt, busily ripping mushrooms out of the soil and replanting them in another patch while talking animatedly to herself the entire time. It seemed like something she probably shouldn't be doing, especially because the little knees of her overalls were all stained with soil, but since she seemed safe enough and I wasn't a parent, I figured it wasn't my business.

I moseyed my way toward one of the tables, passing a large family of gnomes who were arguing about which fruit to take home. The baskets of apples on the tables had little plates laid out in front of them and an older, apron-wearing elvish woman was cutting pieces of fruit as samples for people to try. There were all the usual apple colors—yellows and reds and greens—but there were also interesting dark purple varieties and one basket full of snow-white apples with a pale pink hue around the stem. I drifted closer, entranced by the unique fruit, to find that there were jagged holes in each apple revealing light pink fruit flesh inside.

"Well, hello, miss. You want a bite of the Moon Blush, do you?"

I glanced up to find the elvish woman making her way toward me, before she made a choking sound and stopped in her tracks, fists suddenly clenched tight and the pink in her dark cheeks draining as she stared at the apples.

"Alistair!" she bellowed toward the tree line, startling me. It was *shockingly* brash behavior for an elf, especially an elderly one. "Alistair! That kid's gotten into your basket of Moon Blush apples!"

I had no time to ponder her shouting as a massive mothman—a creature straight out of my darkest cryptid nightmares—stepped out from the darkness of the trees. My jaw dropped at the sight of him. Nearly as tall as a dryad, with a thick, dove-gray lion's mane of fluff and four long, dark arms that seemed to stretch on forever, the creature snapped out a menacing limb with lightning speed and snatched up the little child I'd seen playing with the mushrooms just moments earlier. She screamed like a stuck pig as he hoisted her up, up, up into the air, clutched in his claws by the back of her overalls. My heart lurched into my throat at the sight of her captured by this *monster*. I was not prepared to watch this child die right here!

"Oh, no! Stop!" I barely choked out from across the table, my hands pressed to my cheeks. I felt weak in the knees as he turned to look at me with his lash-lined dark red eyes, frustration and confusion written on every feature. Not the predatory hunger I'd expected from his fearsome mien.

Also unexpected? The little girl's shrieks turning to hysterical, throaty giggles as she reached for one of the fluffy white antennae that arched forward from above his brow. Her dirty fist clutching his strange protuberance jerked his attention away from me, and he squawked at her indignantly.

"Let go," he told her, sounding oddly petulant. Almost *whiny.*

"*You* let go," she said stubbornly, her tiny voice not wavering in the slightest.

"You ate all my apples, Miela!" he insisted, trying to wrestle his antenna from her clutches with two of his many hands, the fourth one gesturing angrily at the box of ruined apples. My racing heart began to slow as I watched the interaction between them, the hammering in my chest easing from sprinting panic to concerned confusion as my hands dropped from my face.

The kid had an iron grip on him as she dangled a good six feet in the air, completely unconcerned about her situation. "I didn't eat all of dem!" she insisted. "I only tasted dem."

He finally managed to pry her hand free, but his antenna was bent oddly and all the little fluffy bits stood askew. "Now look what you've done," he grumbled at her in a low buzz, trying to smooth it back to rights and redirecting her attention to the apples. "Why did you taste every one? I'd have given you a whole apple if you'd asked!"

"I didn't wike dem," she stated matter-of-factly, as if it were the most obvious thing in the world.

"So you just kept *tasting them?*"

As he spoke, his long, thin tongue flickered between his fangs, protruding just enough for the tiny fist he wasn't grasping to dart out and snag it. The outraged yelp he gave as she yanked it toward herself was accompanied by the mothman's frantic buzzing sounds, causing the tiny tot to erupt with further peals of delighted laughter. Her husky giggles were contagious, and seeing that she was manhandling him instead of the other way around caused the relief in my chest to bubble out in my own disbelieving chuckles. I couldn't help it. It was just such an absurd sight, seeing this hulking, furry beast of a monster being worked over so skillfully by this fireball of a toddler. Given how comfortable she was bossing him about, I realized the child must have been his, and I felt silly now for having reacted in fear based on his size and fearsome appearance.

My laughter was a mistake, and I cringed internally as he followed the sound of it to stare at me glumly, his tongue still pulled taut from the side of his mouth by the child. "I'm so sorry," I stuttered out, suddenly horribly embarrassed by my earlier outburst when I'd thought he was going to harm her. "I didn't realize she was yours!" My cheeks were hot as I raised my hands again, this time holding them in front of me in a placating gesture in the hopes that he would disregard my previous panic. Even though I was still mildly panicking as he turned his focus on me. Those eyes made the prickling feeling on the back of my neck feel like pins and needles.

The mothman reached out to pry his tubular tongue from the toddler's grip, never taking his eyes off of me, all the while. She giggled again as his tongue was freed, but I couldn't remove my gaze from the dark-fringed, red eyes he had trained on me, wearing a decidedly unimpressed expression.

"Mine? Like my child?" he asked incredulously, his wings flaring dramatically as his voice moved from its buzzy rumble into a higher octave. *Oh, no.* "She might only be a quarter orc, but look at these tusks!" He wiggled her in the air with the hand that gripped her scruff, causing her to squeal with laughter again as her pigtails bounced to and fro. She did, indeed, have the tiniest of tusks peeking above her bottom lip. My eyes snapped back to the mothman. "Mothchildren haven't even got any *bones*," he continued indignantly, "let alone teeth."

"I have teef!" the little one declared cheerfully, opening her mouth to show them to everyone as I glanced at her quickly.

But the mothman wasn't finished as he continued in a huff. "I know you elves must think every green child is a caterbaby, but she hasn't even got the right number of limbs!" He sounded positively perturbed, and I didn't know what to think, so I just apologized profusely for the assumption and started to retreat slowly from the table, my hands still held aloft. The child was clearly fine, and I needed to make an escape. I would just send Artem to buy whatever trees he thought would sell well.

"Sir, are these mushrooms for sale?" An oblivious old goblin man stepped up next to me with a ceramic pot full of the same mushrooms the tusked toddler had been digging up earlier.

"My mushwooms!" she squealed, darting her hands out toward the pot as if she could snatch them back from the man.

"The low-fae are not for sale," the mothman stated sternly. "They go wherever they want. Miela," he said, addressing his tiny captive, "you have to stop pulling them up or they'll bite you."

"They bite?" the old man asked in a bewildered tone, blinking down at the little red and white fungi.

"You, come with me," the mothman instructed, pointing one of his many long-clawed fingers at me.

I froze in my tracks, five steps away from the table already. So much for sneaking away. "Who, me?" I gestured at my chest, my eyes wide in panic. "Oh, no. No, sir. I'm good... I'm just gonna—" I started to gesture over my shoulder, indicating that I would head back the way I came, but he cut me off.

"You wanted to try a Moon Blush, didn't you? Come this way. These are my best apples, if I do say so myself. You'll never be the same once you try one. You *simply* haven't lived." He snapped his enormous gray wings together forcefully, leaving a shimmering mote of dust behind him as he ducked into his grove of trees. He shifted his hold on the little girl to carry her against his chest while she howled loudly about wanting her mushrooms back.

The little old man continued to stand next to me, staring at the little pot of strange fungus he held. "These are low-fae?" he asked aloud, though he sounded like he was speaking to himself.

Suddenly, the elderly elvish woman was there, gently taking the pot from him. "Best to put those down or that little girl's mother will have your hide, Arnold. Miss," she said, waving me toward the trees, "you go follow Alistair now, and he'll get you some of those pretty apples. They're our most popular," she said with pride.

I had just wanted to look at them! Augh! I practically stomped around the table and ducked into the first row of trees, immediately aware of how dim the light was under the low canopy of leaves. Hadn't my mother always warned me about stranger-danger? Wasn't it unsafe to go off into the woods? Granted, the tidy rows of neatly pruned apple trees could hardly be termed "woods," but I thought the same principle should apply. I was a city-girl through and through. I could just imagine myself getting lost in the orchard and wandering for hours. I'd never live it down if my uncle heard about it.

Fortunately, it wasn't hard to follow the arguing duo—Alistair and Miela, I reminded myself—as they bickered and squabbled on their way down the rows of trees. The toddler wanted down, and the mothman wasn't having any of it. "No! You lost your walking privileges," he stated when she squirmed in his many arms. "If you can't make good choices, then you have to stay with me." She quieted as he stopped at a tree laden with glossy white fruit, just beginning to show the pink hue at their tops, and reached clear into the upper branches to pluck one off.

"I want one," she squeaked.

"You've had plenty," he muttered, barely loud enough for me to hear as I tripped over my own feet in my effort to catch up to him. I tried to hide my stumbling misstep as he turned to face me, towering over me as I drew nearer. His large silhouette against the canopy above cut a menacing figure, but something about the copious tufts of soft-looking fluff covering his chest and body reminded me of a silk moth. His eyes had become a muted maroon color under the shadowed leaves, much less shocking than the brilliant crimson they'd projected in the late afternoon sun. The long dark fringes surrounding them—as well as the tiny child held carefully in his arms—softened him somehow. I was still unsure of him, but the absent way he rubbed circles between the girl's shoulder blades as she began to suck her thumb and snuggled into his fluff melted my anxiety clean away.

I raised my gaze to meet his when he hesitated with the apple in his hand, holding it carefully with the pads of his fingers so that his sharp, black claws didn't mar the perfect skin. His feathered antennae bobbled above his head, and his expression appeared uncertain. "These are my favorites," he said in his rumbling buzz. "But it's okay if you don't like it." He extended the apple to me slowly, as if he was aware of my nerves, and I took it carefully from him, marveling over the glossy texture. Alistair's head seemed to shrink into the mounds of fluff around it as he hitched his shoulders up to his ears. I didn't understand the gesture since there was no way a creature like this could be *shy*.

"Should we take it back to the tables so the lady can cut it up and share it?" I asked, glancing back to where the evening sun still played at the edges of the trees.

"I can get more," he answered quietly with a descending click, his fluff levitating even higher around his ears. "I want you to have it."

Chapter 2

Lilith

I BOUGHT FIVE TREES, which was all he had available: four to resell at the nursery and one for myself. The fruit was unlike anything I could purchase at any grocery store, and I just knew I'd want one of the sapling trees to take home with me to my little patio garden at my condo in New Caelora. The trees themselves were rather unremarkable—they looked like any other apple tree—but that fruit! Sweet, fresh, crisp, and perfectly tart with an almost tropical undertone… I didn't understand how this mothman hadn't flooded the market with his new creation. I made a promise to myself to go back to the orchard and buy a box of those apples as soon as I could. I knew how hard rare fruits could be to source, and it would be a few years before my new little tree would start producing.

For now, I'd placed my baby tree in a beautiful cement planter in front of my largest apartment window. It was a little bright spot of joy for me whenever I was in my cramped, dimly lit apartment, and it cheered me up every time I looked at it. At least, it did in the beginning.

I couldn't put my finger on it, but it just seemed... unhappy somehow. *"Do plants have feelings?"* one might ask. Well, not in the same way we do, but those of us with plant magic had long accepted that there was something there that we could feel when a plant was thriving in an optimum environment that was missing when it was not. And little by little this young tree that brightened up my dull apartment living room was slowly losing its "happy." That was the best way I could translate the feeling it gave me.

I then watched with dismay as my "feeling" was confirmed when the leaves began to yellow and drop over the following weeks. It was especially disappointing because I've always had a knack with plants. Having a green thumb is one of my defining characteristics! I could intuitively tell what they needed or what they would tolerate, and this sapling tree should have been just fine in an appropriately sized pot with plenty of sunlight and an appropriate amount of water and nutrients. Instead of joy, the plant quickly became a source of disappointment. It was a hit to my ego to have failed this plant. I was sad for the plant that it wasn't doing well, and I was embarrassed for myself that I'd potentially ruined one of that mothman's prized trees. I even asked Artem what he was doing differently with the trees in our shop greenhouse, but he didn't have any suggestions for me other than the small amount of dryad magic he lent them every time he watered. I considered plying him with beer or whatever dryads drank to come give my tree a boost of his magic, but even the trees in his care weren't doing as well as they had been for the mothman. He'd told me to just give it time.

I babied it. Checked its water level every day. Inspected it for pests. Offered it extra humidity. Less humidity. Some organic plant food. Moved the pot slightly for more optimum sunlight.

Eventually, I decided to just leave it alone and hope for the best, but every time I walked by it, I felt my anxiety rise as I inevitably scanned it for more signs of distress. So, you'd think I would have noticed when little buds started to protrude from the soil in the pot, but somehow, I missed it.

It wasn't until multiple little red fungus tops were poking from the soil that I noticed their growth, stopping in my tracks one day as I passed through my living room. There they were, little white stems with red tops clustered in the dirt. Great, I thought to myself. More evidence that the tree is dying. The roots were probably rotting. I reached for the soil to test if it was over-saturated and nearly came out of my skin when one of the mushrooms turned and *looked at me*. It didn't do anything else, just blinked up at me with its beady little black eyes and then returned to its original position.

"What the hell?" I said aloud, quiet as a breath. The mushroom didn't react. I had a whole-ass mushroom-person colony living in my house. I squatted down to get a better look—while keeping my distance—recognizing them as the same type that the little girl had been pulling up and repotting at the apple orchard. My soil must have been contaminated. The mothman had called them low-fae and told the old man holding a pot of them that they would bite.

One of the mushrooms toward the back of the cluster peeked up at me from under its little cap, and I narrowed my eyes at it. It immediately hid its face again and froze.

I'd heard of low-fae, but I'd never seen one before, not like this anyway. Did I want biting low-fae in my house? No, I did not... but aside from carrying the tree out to the dumpster in its concrete pot, how was I supposed to get them out? Trap them in a cup like a spider? Could they even move around? Were they damaging my tree?

Watching for any sign of movement out of the corner of my vision, I finally pried my eyes off of the toadstools and took stock of my tree. It seemed... greener. The leaves looked better than they had since I brought it home. And now that I was paying attention, it had that spark of thriving I could feel in my magic. For the first time in weeks, I began to hope that it might pull through. And the only thing that had changed were these weird little mushrooms. I eyed them again, considering. If they were making the tree healthier... and they weren't hurting anything... I squinted at them and thought about poking one of them to see how it reacted, but I was afraid of getting bitten. That little girl hadn't been harmed, though.

I watched them for a while longer and eventually decided that I would leave them alone—as long as they stayed in the pot and my tree didn't show any signs of damage. But at the first sign of any movement outside of the pot, I was going to catch them with some kitchen tongs and a bucket and throw them outside.

THE MUSHROOMS NEVER MOVED as I checked them obsessively for the rest of the day. None of them even twitched or acknowledged my presence, so I started to question my sanity and whether I'd actually seen them move at all, but I wasn't brave enough to poke one and see if it reacted. Every time I peeked in on them, I felt like I was intruding, but I was nervous about them being in my home. When bedtime finally came, I still felt uneasy, but finally retreated to my bedroom—after snooping another three times to make sure they hadn't moved.

Enveloped in darkness, I lay in bed, listening to the scritch, scritch, scritch of my upstairs neighbor's claws as he moved about his apartment, wallowing in my discontent. I missed my friends. I missed my street and the familiar faces at the coffee shop down the block from my condo. The barista with the cheerful smile and my regular drink order waiting for me every morning. My favorite little elvish cafe with the locally sourced potted pies that always hit the spot on chilly nights. There were elvish pies here, I'd found, but they didn't taste the same, and I'd spent hours combing the local shops unsuccessfully for my favorite starlight tea. I missed being able to rescue my uncle from yet another plant-sales-based mishap. Going out for drinks with my friends from college on a random Friday night. My morning routine of coffee with Melantha, the cousin who was filling in for me. I loved the familiar comfort of sipping our drinks as I pored over the previous day's paperwork, while she filled me in on how her parents were doing or what her new husband was up to at the kinesthetics clinic for wyverns, where he was completing his internship. Even just joking around with Jaque, the new kid we'd hired to work the sales floor since I'd moved into management. None of that existed here, and I felt so disconnected. I could send them messages through the network of spectral messengers, but it wasn't the same as interacting with them and just quietly existing alongside them.

There was no one to talk to here, or spend my days alongside. That whole sense of family—of community—was missing. Now, Artem was fine. He was a fantastic employee. He just didn't joke around or feel much of a need to engage outside of business-related discussions. Which was fine! Yet, the end result was that I felt a little out of sorts unless Jereck was around, and he only worked part time. How had I gone from being annoyed by his constant chatter to enjoying his shifts?

I was lonely and felt out of place, I admitted to myself. I didn't feel like I fit in here, and I didn't know that I wanted to. This wasn't my home, after all—I wasn't planning on staying. I'd obviously known that coming in and thought I was prepared for it, but the longer I was here, the more adrift I felt. By the time I fell asleep that night, I was resolved to work my butt off to make the new plant shop profitable as soon as possible. I would prove that I could do it—I would make my uncle proud—and then I could get the heck back to New Caelora. Back to my real home.

TWO WEEKS WENT BY without any change or movement from my new mushroom roommates, who only occasionally opened their eyes to glance at me when I stared at them like a loon. I wouldn't have even known they were there if I hadn't spotted them, and over time, especially as my tree grew noticeably more healthy—still not robust by any means, but I took what I could get—I decided I didn't really mind their presence. I didn't know how sentient they were, but it became weirdly comforting having them there after a while.

None of the trees at the greenhouse had shown any sign of soil contamination or low-fae growth, and Artem had just given a grumpy shrug and continued packing dirt into some seed-starting trays when I asked if he knew anything about low-fae growing in plants. My bafflement continued.

And then, one night, I walked by on my way to bed and stopped in my tracks, slopping steaming chamomile tea over the side of my cup and all over the scuffed hardwood floor in front of me. Because there was a *frog* in my apple tree pot, nestled down among the mushrooms.

"No," I said aloud to no one in particular. "We're not doing this." No more extraneous creatures living in my house.

Abandoning what was left of my cup of tea to the sideboard table, I reached for the frog. Heedless of the toadstools, I brushed right past them and scooped him up. He was slimy and bumpy, and his little body was cold in my hand, but I refused to allow myself to gag. *I really wanted to gag.* We marched right out the front door and down the hall to the stairs—me in my flannel pants, oversized sleep shirt, and bunny slippers, and frog in his slimy frog-ness. And then I full-body-*slammed* into a warm, fluffy wall of heat and muscle as I jogged out the door at the bottom of the stairs on my way out.

The frog leapt from my hands as I startled backward, choking on my fear as bright red eyes filled my vision. A piercing shriek rang out as the towering mothman recoiled away from me. A window opened several stories above.

"Hey, shut up! We're sleeping here!" yelled an annoyed voice before the window slammed shut again. I cringed. The mothman cringed. The frog probably cringed, wherever he was. Apartment Etiquette 101: Respect the Quiet Hours.

Alistair's antennae were flattened against his head, and all four arms were pulled tightly against his body as he practically cowered away from me with a chastened-sounding chirp. Above us, an old gooseneck lamp illuminated the entryway, its flickering light catching the mothman's enormous ruby colored eyes and making them look like they were glowing from within. I took a deep breath, and—realizing I wasn't being attacked from the darkness by some *monster*—asked the only question my brain could lock onto at the moment.

"Was that your high-pitched shriek?"

My question seemed to bring him back to himself. "You startled me." His answer was clipped and carried an irritated buzz as he straightened up and began dusting off his front with all four of his hands. Dust motes sparkled in the lamplight as they flew off his feathery chest and mane. I looked down at myself to see that I was also covered in sparkly dust. That hadn't been there when I'd left my apartment.

"I'm sorry," I responded quickly, awkwardly scrubbing at the dust coating my shirt with my wrists since my hands were coated in frog goo. What on earth? Moth dust? "What—what are you doing here?" I asked him.

"I live here," he said with an affronted air, before slowly beginning to return to his cringing pose as he took in my flailing attempts to remove the glittery substance from my clothes. It almost looked like he was wilting. "I fear our wing scales are not that easily removed from clothing."

I stopped the awkward scrubbing, not wanting to embarrass him. "It's fine," I assured him. Surely it would launder out. I was the one who had run into him, after all. "Were you just... standing here?" I asked, pointing at the ground like a dummy, still confused by the entirety of the last few minutes. There was no sign of the frog I'd brought outside. Alistair didn't respond for several beats, so I looked up from where I was searching the ground to find him frowning at me.

"I like the lamp," he finally answered.

"You're just out here lurking under the lamp?" I asked. My brain caught up as I remembered the red eyes in the windows above my apartment and the tapping of talons on my ceiling all night. *He lives here?* A quick glance at his feet revealed that he did indeed have long, sharp talons on powerful looking bird-like feet. Alistair was my upstairs neighbor.

My brain had a hard time keeping up as I processed this information. I found myself allowing my eyes to scan his form, wondering what else I had failed to notice the day I met him as I'd scrambled after him through the orchard. His legs had a backward turned hock in the same way a bird or horse does, and sturdy looking thighs led up to well-defined abdominal muscles that gave my stomach a fluttery feeling as I stared at them. His chest and shoulders held bulky muscles used for powering the massive wings he currently had folded tightly behind him. His limbs and body were covered in a soft, velvety down that was darker in color than the puffy mane of fluff around his neck. Right now, with his shoulders hunched, he looked like he was trying to disappear into his fluff. It occurred to me that he was oddly... cute. I felt my lips curve up.

"I'm... I'm not lurking," he stammered, his tiny fangs making an appearance as he spoke. "I just appreciate a nice lamp when I see one."

"Okay." I heard the confusion in my own voice and bit back my amusement, not wanting to offend him further. "Well... enjoy, I guess." I flashed him a quick smile and reached behind me to open the door, mentally apologizing to my neighbors for the frog goo I left on the doorknob. I wasn't coming back down tonight to wipe it off and risking another strange encounter of the mothman kind.

As I was turning off the sink in my kitchen, I heard the familiar tick, tick, tick of claws in front of my apartment and tiptoed to the door to peek through the peephole. Sure enough, Alistair passed in front of my unit and down the hall toward the rear set of stairs to the upper floor. Several minutes later, his tapping claws sounded through the ceiling above.

As I climbed into bed that night, something inside me relaxed for the first time since I'd come here. The scritch, scritch, scritch was suddenly familiar instead of foreign, now that I knew who it was, and I wondered what he was doing up there. I pictured him dusting a shelf or tidying his apartment. Maybe he had a plant. I had difficulty imagining him doing the same mundane household chores that the rest of us participated in—maybe he wore a blue gingham apron while he dusted his apartment with a fluffy, white feather duster that matched his antennae, or perhaps he had two sets of matching pink dish gloves to protect his perfectly sharp claws while he did the washing up—but the effort of doing so tugged a small smile to my lips and lifted a bit of the heaviness that had been collecting in my chest over the last several weeks.

I'd changed my shirt but had been too tired to take another shower, and the scent of his scales still blanketed me as I lay in bed. Soft, warm musk and crisp night air. I wondered why I hadn't seen him around the apartment before. I'd seen the middle-aged elvish man who lived next door as he came and went, and the younger goblin in her stylish, pressed suits who lived across the hall, along with several others as we were coming and going, but never the mothman.

I realized as I drifted off to sleep that he must be nocturnal. I wondered if he had any friends, or if he was lonely. Like me.

Chapter 3

Lilith

The frog was back. Or maybe it was a different frog. I don't know how, or why, or when, but two days later, there was a frog in my planter.

I took it outside again, scolding it the entire way, and this time I made sure to deposit it a little more carefully, placing it under some bushes on the far side of the building property. Then I came back inside and searched the entire apartment, looking for any opening that it could have gotten in through. All the air vents were secure and the windows—though they all had paint peeling from the sills and creaky locks—were closed up tight as well. My doors were fitted tightly with no spaces something could enter through. The apartment was certainly old and in need of renovation, but there were no obvious gaps anywhere that I could find. There was nothing.

I had frogs magically appearing in my living room.

Maybe they were coming out of the planter? But I had planted that tree myself and had broken up the root ball and checked it for anything "off" the same way I've always done for every plant I've re-potted. It made no sense.

The next day, there was another frog. "What is going on?" I practically yelled at the frog. He was half buried in the damp potting soil, his little backside dug into the substrate, placidly sitting there with his little froggy eyes giving a thousand-yard stare. This was out of control.

I scooped him up and examined him. Now, I'm no frog-ologist, but I was pretty sure this was the same frog. It had the same toady little body, the same coloring, the same warty little bumps on its head and shoulders. His eyes were buggy and giving major "no thoughts, just frog" vibes, and his throat pouch was going a mile a minute, but he didn't struggle in my hands at all. "You can't keep doing this," I told him. "My house is not the place for you. I don't have frog food. There are no ponds for you to sit in. I'm going to come in here one day and find your desiccated little frog body dried out in my pot. Nobody wants that," I explained to him.

I carried him outside and deposited him farther away this time before continuing on to work, where I scrubbed my hands until I thought my skin might come off.

Later that day, I asked, "Artem, have you ever had a frog just show up inside your house?"

The old man paused with the watering can he held and looked at me like I was crazy. "Why would a frog show up inside my house?"

"I don't know! I keep finding a frog in my house."

"The same frog?" he asked incredulously.

"I think so," I responded with uncertainty.

He continued to stare at me like I was crazy, so I let it drop. "Never mind." I waved him off, and he shuffled away to return to his tasks, leaving me to finish balancing the books.

And then the frog was there, waiting for me, when I returned home that evening. And I had absolutely had enough. I had begged. I'd scolded. I'd pleaded. I'd threatened. I had *implored* it to stay out of my house. Did I know that talking to a frog, magical or not, was nonsense? Yes. Did I do it anyway? Also yes.

What else was I going to find in my house next? If a frog could get in, what else could? I also didn't want it to die of starvation or dehydration, which seemed inevitable if it managed to stay inside without me noticing it.

But Frog didn't listen.

Frog never left.

Frog was eternal.

Frog was determined to live in my plant pot.

But my plant pot already had plenty of unwelcome guests making it home—*I'm looking at you, fungi friends*—and so I scooped the toady menace up again and marched it right back outside.

How far away does one need to take a frog to keep it from returning to the same place?

Alistair

MY NEIGHBOR WAS IN a tree.

I'd smelled the perfume of her skin long before I arrived, that beguiling scent that had plagued me every night since she moved in as I worked among my plants. Splicing and budding and grafting my trees in my home was supposed to be a peaceful experience for me, but the scent of her living below me made me restless. My antennae itched with how much I enjoyed it, and I frowned at her, perched as she was in the sprawling branches of an old royal ibec tree in a field down the road from our building. I'd always appreciated the unique texture of its bark, myself.

I halted my flight to work, landing along the walkway to take a closer look at her confusing behavior. Rubbing at the base of my antenna, trying to scrub away her scent and free myself from her thrall, I thought about whether to approach. I had left a very exciting project in my lab—a scion I was trying to graft with a new technique!—and I wanted to see if the splint had held. I spread my wings to continue on my way... and then slowly folded them back again.

Why was my neighbor in the tree? I didn't think elvish people—or whatever she was; I wasn't particularly well-versed in the non-forest races—were tree-dwelling people. The elves I knew all tended to prefer bigger cities and more urban environments than I had much experience with, but maybe this one had a penchant for tree climbing. The way she was sprawled awkwardly within the branches, not even gripping one with her—admittedly very few—forelimbs made me doubt that she had any kind of arboreal adeptness.

I glanced forlornly in the direction of my laboratory, but I knew that my incessant curiosity and predilection for imagining the worst-case scenarios in every situation would keep me from being able to focus on my tasks without first ascertaining the well-being of this aromatically enticing neighbor. *Sigh.*

Picking my way across the poorly mown grass and doing my best to ignore the overly prickly feeling of the thick, rough blades between the sensitive pads of my feet, I studied the woman as I approached. Her skin was a warm golden brown, and her chin-length hair a deep chestnut with a hint of red showing in the setting sun. Her face was very expressive—an endearing trait to someone such as me without as many malleable features—clearly broadcasting her frustration and discomfort at the moment. Eyes the same reddish-chestnut color tracked my progress across the damp, horrible lawn. I could have flown, yes, but her precarious position in the branches made me loathe to risk startling her and causing her to slip.

"Hello, there," I called to her.

"Hi," she responded in an oddly squeaky tone. Her cheeks flushed pink immediately. She was stretched forward across two larger limbs, her legs awkwardly braced to keep her from falling, but instead of holding on to the branches as seemed appropriate for a wingless creature, she was cupping her hands in front of her and resting her elbow as another point of contact on the branch. I never did understand how these people survived with so few forelimbs.

"Do you require assistance?" I asked her, half hoping she did not so that I could see to my scions that much more quickly.

Curiously, the pink in her cheeks deepened to a ruddier hue. "Uh... Possibly. I mean, maybe? I don't suppose you have a ladder?" She gave a small, self-deprecating laugh.

I stared at her for a beat longer than I should have, trying to make sense of her question. I'd never had need of a ladder in my life, but the ground-dwelling races obviously used them when they needed to ascend something tall that had no stairs. Perhaps a nearby construction project would have a ladder, but I didn't really need one to get her down when I could fly.

"I'm stuck," she clarified.

"I see that," I assured her. "Unfortunately, I do not own a ladder. However, I am prepared to assist you down, if you would like," I offered.

"Oh, no. I'm afraid if you climb up here it will shake the branches and I'll fall." Her voice trembled slightly as she spoke.

Perhaps she assumed that the wings on my back were purely for aesthetic purposes. If I could have rolled my eyes in my head, I would have. Alas, I could not—I'd always been envious of that ability—so I snapped my wings out dramatically instead and gestured to them with all four hands. "I have no need to climb the tree. I can easily fly up and retrieve you."

"I don't... I don't think that's a good idea," she said with another short laugh, this one sounding incredibly nervous. "I'm not exactly pixie-sized, right? I've got thighs for days and a booty to match," she said with another strange-sounding laugh. "Don't worry about it, I'll figure something out," she finished half-heartedly.

Did she think I couldn't lift her? It was true that she didn't have the slender build most common to the elvish people, instead possessing a rounded softness that I found rather pleasing, personally. But unless she was made of lead, it was rather insulting to imply that I couldn't support such a small weight. I could carry a full-grown orc if I wanted to. "Miss—"

"Lilith," she supplied quickly. "My name is Lilith."

I nodded. A beautiful name. "Miss Lilith, I have a fourteen-foot wingspan." I gestured to my wings again and flared them to their fullest spread, feeling the bases of my antennae heat with embarrassment at such a forward display. "I can assure you that it would not be a problem to lift you down."

To my confusion, she shrank back slightly, closer to the trunk of the tree, clearly uncomfortable with the idea.

"Or—" I paused to think. "—I can summon emergency services?" I offered, having no desire to pressure her. "I'm sure they would have a ladder and experience with retrieving wayward elves from ibec trees."

"Oh, no," she gasped, "please don't bother them with this. That's so embarrassing. I'm fine. I'll just... I'm sure I can figure out how to get down," she babbled, her fear evident in her voice. She shifted slightly on the branch, glanced down, and then promptly froze again.

The odds of her climbing down without the use of her hands seemed incredibly dubious to me. Instead of lifting her down, as would be easiest, I decided to join her in the tree. "I'm coming up," I warned her, then beat my wings in short, forceful strokes, just enough to lift myself off the ground. Angling between a gap in the branches where I could settle myself on a nearby limb, I used my taloned feet to grip carefully close to the trunk so as not to dislodge her from her perch. Her alluring scent had clung to my densely feathered mane after she ran into me a few evenings ago, and it was overwhelming again this close to her. Her alarmed expression quickly calmed as I shifted my weight away from her to show that I wasn't planning to snatch her out of the tree but was simply joining her. The freckles across her nose and cheekbones, which I'd noticed while staring at her under the lamplight before, were barely visible in the shadows of the tree.

"If I join you up here," I started to explain, "then I can see to instruct you on the best footholds to climb down. Though if I may suggest, it seems like the use of your hands would be beneficial."

"I can't. I've got a frog." She said it as though that were all the explanation required.

"A frog," I prompted, after it became clear that was all she was going to say on the matter.

"Yeah. In my hands. I brought it out here," she nodded at the field below us, "because I'm tired of it coming into my house, so I figured this was far enough away, you know? But then a crow snatched it up and flew up here to eat it, alive, and I can't be responsible for that. It'd be my fault it was dead!" She clamped her mouth shut, grimacing as she realized she had been babbling again.

"So, you... climbed the tree?" I asked.

"I... Yes... Because the bird dropped the frog when I chased it, and it got caught in the crook of this branch on the way down. I couldn't leave it like that. I felt so bad."

"And now you're stuck, because you're holding the frog," I surmised.

"That, and I didn't realize how high up I was until I looked down." Her voice took on a slightly higher pitch.

"Ah," I said, things finally clicking into place. "So you're afraid of heights."

"Um, yes. Yeah. That probably seems so silly to someone who can fly. This is so embarrassing. I can't believe I climbed up here."

I tried to give my most soothing hum from deep in my thorax. "I think it was very brave to climb up here, if you were afraid. We all have our fears. I'm afraid of lots of things that would probably seem silly to you."

She shifted the weight of her legs on the tree branch, obviously uncomfortable with the way it was digging into her knee, but as she did, she looked down and froze in fear again.

I kept talking, trying to distract her but struggling to come up with something suitable. "I'm afraid of... um... gum," I said, frowning slightly as I realized what I'd just said.

But it worked.

She jerked her gaze to me and gave a few rapid blinks. "You're afraid of chewing gum?" she asked doubtfully.

"I am," I affirmed with a nod. "It's sticky and awful. Imagine getting it stuck in my fluff," I explained, stroking the feathers of my mane with a hand. "It happened once, thanks to the same small child you witnessed terrorizing my orchard," I explained. Miela had gotten a wad of it stuck in my mane one time and it had taken her mother, Solandis, over an hour to get it out using peanut butter. We'd nearly had to cut it out, and I would have spent months walking around with a hole in my mane. Gum was horrible stuff. "It is now firmly off-limits around my person," I said with a huff, causing her to give me a flicker of a bemused smile. I wanted to punch the air with pride at having managed to draw out even the smallest of smiles from her in her distressed state, but I refrained and searched instead for something else with which to distract her.

"Oh, and angler fish," I stated, suddenly remembering how horrifying they looked. I sat back further on my own branch, trying to get comfortable while I waited for my companion's nerves to continue to calm. It was strangely enjoyable watching her expressions as she mentally parsed through her reactions to my announced fears.

Confused amusement was what she landed on. "Why would you be afraid of angler fish?" she asked curiously. "Have you ever even seen one in person?"

I huffed at her and crossed my upper arms. "Of course not. Since they can't survive out of the deep ocean and I cannot swim, I doubt I'll ever meet one face to face. Can you imagine me swimming?" I gestured at my wings and the sheer amount of poofy fuzz covering my body. "I would look like a drowned rat," I informed her. If I'd had a nose, I would have raised it in the air at the thought of such a disgraceful image. I hated being wet. It was the worst.

She gave me another confused smile, still not understanding. "Then why..." She let her question trail off.

"I've seen pictures of them, and that's enough for me. The mere concept of angler fish is terrifying. Just imagine being down in the deep, dark ocean and suddenly coming upon a lovely little glowing lamp. You excitedly swim over to check out such an exquisite find, and then GIANT NEEDLE TEETH EMERGE FROM THE DARKNESS!" It was the ultimate betrayal. I might have gotten a little loud and dramatic, considering Lilith burst into laughter at my narration. Working to lower my voice, I concluded, "Truly the stuff of nightmares."

Her smile was wide as she settled a little more comfortably beside me. The sound of her laughter made my chest feel jittery, and I decided I needed to hear more of it. I cast about mentally for something else to make her laugh.

"What is your most ridiculous fear? I bet I can top it," I challenged.

"I can't really think of a ridiculous one," she answered slowly. "Unless you count the fear of heights," she said, glancing down as she said it.

"No!" That was not what I wanted. "It only counts if it can't actually harm you." Back to silly topics and not the drop below her. I would never allow her to fall. I could reach out and snatch her back in an instant, but doing so might injure her delicate skin if I weren't able to be as careful as I wanted with my claws. Better to calm her nerves and discuss a safer way to get her down, one that she consented to and felt safe with.

"Um, I don't know. Death? Dying?"

I scoffed. "You're terrible at this game."

"How about... monsters," she decided, enunciating slowly and looking at me out of the corner of her eye. "I guess... those aren't even real... so it's a ridiculous fear."

"Hm, I suppose," I conceded, scooting closer to her. Many people would consider me a monster, for some bizarre reason—probably because they felt inadequate due to their limited number of arms—but if she didn't, then I felt no need to correct her. Time to implement my plan. "How about I take your frog from you, and then your hands will be free to grip the branch?" I held out one of my hands toward her, still able to hold on to the tree with five other perfectly useful appendages, trying not to convey my smugness at how superior mothpeople's bodies were.

Lilith frowned at my hand. "He's slimy," she warned me, glancing back at my face.

I couldn't keep my own frown from mirroring hers. Slime in the velvety covering on my hands was utterly dreadful. I sighed and wiggled my fingers at her to encourage her to give up the frog.

She did, albeit hesitantly, gripping the plump little body carefully as she slowly reached to deposit the creature into my hand. I closed my fingers around it just as carefully and drew it closer to study it.

"He looks familiar," I muttered. "Is this Patrick?"

She paused while scrubbing the palm of her hand off on the bark of the unsuspecting tree and blinked at me. "I wasn't aware frogs have names."

"Why wouldn't they have names?"

"I don't know. It just started showing up in my apple tree pot around the same time that those little low-fae mushrooms from your orchard began growing in it."

"Then it's probably Patrick," I decided. This silly git was friends with some of the mushrooms that my friend Solandis had encouraged to infest my orchard, claiming the little biters helped my trees. He was always getting himself into a pickle. "You said he was inside your house?" I asked, trying to distract her again. "See if you can put your toe on the ridge of that bark, there on the trunk," I suggested, pointing to the spot where I thought she had the greatest chance of attaining traction.

"Um, yes," she confirmed as she carefully focused on simultaneously answering my question, following my suggestion, and not on looking at the ground, as I had hoped. "Do you know how he gets in? I've checked everywhere."

"I haven't the slightest idea." I didn't even know how he could have gotten there from the orchard. But maybe the mushrooms just hung out with any old frog? "Can you reach that limb there?" I asked as I pointed. Dropping from the limb I had perched on, I lowered myself to be able to get a better vantage point.

"I think so," she replied, her voice a little shaky again.

"You're doing fantastically. Just look at me—no, don't look down, focus on me—I won't let you get hurt," I encouraged, producing the most soothing buzz I knew and keeping a hand close to her so she had a safe place to grab onto if she needed. Her tremulous smile made my heart beat faster. I hadn't paid enough attention to notice how pretty she was before this evening, or perhaps her smile simply amplified her beauty so much that I couldn't miss it.

She did take hold of my hand as she climbed, startling me enough that I had lost the train of the conversation when she asked, "Is he fae?"

"Pardon?" I asked, trying to ignore the swarm of moth wings beating frantically in my chest.

"The frog," she clarified, reminding me of the slimy little body in my hand that I'd conveniently forgotten about. She leaned more of her weight onto my hand and bravely reached for another branch with her foot. "You said the mushrooms were low-fae. Is the frog fae too?"

"Oh, no. I've never seen a frog-fae. Though if you see one of the jackalopes around here, that's a fae."

She stumbled into me as I helped to lower her onto the ground. "Jackalopes are real?" She asked incredulously. "Wha—what about other cryptids? Is Bigfoot real?"

"Of course," I assured her, helping to steady her and checking her over to make sure she was unharmed. Bigfoot was the name of one of the members of a group of brown forest yetis, but he was certainly real. As my friend Jordan would say, Bigfoot was a real dick. And he was sorely lacking in personal hygiene. But that wasn't what she'd asked.

Lilith blinked at me rapidly, and then her surroundings, finally realizing she was safely on the ground. "Thank you," she said, her voice pitching high again as she released my hand and stepped back. I immediately regretted the loss, but withdrew my hand as well.

"We did it!" she exclaimed, turning to look at the tree before fixing me with her gaze. "But you never told me what your most ridiculous fear is."

I'd already forgotten my impulsive challenge. Sigh. "Bugs," I admitted, steeling myself for her reaction.

She jerked her head back, clearly startled by my confession. "Bugs? But you're—"

"Not a bug," I clarified haughtily, straightening one of my antennae that had become absurdly mussed in the branches. "I may appear similarly built to an insect, but it's called 'convergent evolution.' You can look it up."

Half a dozen reactions flickered across her features again before she settled on incredulity. "You're afraid of all bugs? Or just certain ones?"

"I dislike most of them immensely," I hedged, "but cicadas are the worst with their incessant screaming." Bees and other pollinators were tolerable due to their work for my beloved fruit trees. No amount of hand pollinating could compare to the natural course of things, no matter how many hands I had.

Lilith wrinkled her nose, highlighting the delightful freckles dappled across its dainty bridge, and let her head dip, trying not to laugh. I was taken by the way her hair skimmed across her cheek bones. "They are pretty creepy," she agreed, "but they're only singing their love songs with their butts." She erupted into a fit of laughter so forceful that I found myself beaming at her entirely against my will, as if she had drawn my mouth into an involuntary grin. She was adorable.

Silence began to stretch, and she cleared her throat. I straightened quickly, realizing I was listing toward her slightly, entranced by her warmth and good cheer. There was no reason to stay any longer, as she was safely on the ground and I was free to take Patrick back to the orchard. But I found myself desiring to prolong our contact.

"I should probably find a better place to release the frog—"

"How are your—"

We both spoke over each other and then stopped. She blinked at me and rolled her lips in to bite them, embarrassed.

"Pardon me," I apologized for interrupting her. "Seeing as my hand is already sullied with amphibian secretions," I paused to heft the slight weight of his cool, damp body in my hand, "I might as well take him back to the orchard on my way to the office. There is no danger of crows finding him there," I assured her. The mushrooms would see to that. Vicious little creatures.

"Oh! That would be lovely, thank you."

I flashed her a wistful smile as I accepted that our interaction was over and stepped away, lifting the frog toward her as an awkward parting wave.

She stopped me. "Oh, wait, was there something you were going to ask me just now?" Her face looked curiously hopeful when I turned back to her.

My antennae flushed hot again as I took in another whiff of her pleasant scent. Whatever that was, she should bottle it up and sell it. I wracked my brain, trying to remember my question. "Oh, yes! I was going to ask how your trees were doing?" I was still feeling smug that she'd liked my Moon Blush apples enough to buy out all the rest of the bare root stock of our four-foot semi-dwarf saplings.

The curious hope immediately drained from her expression.

Chapter 4

Lilith

UNFOLDING AND REFOLDING MY felted wool blanket for the fourth time didn't make it lay any nicer across the back of my threadbare, rented couch. No matter how I tried to fix it, it just didn't look nice. I knew I was fixating, but I was still kicking myself over the previous day's embarrassment of getting myself stuck in a tree. And why couldn't I have just *lied* when Alistair asked how my tree was doing? I'd told him the truth, like an absolute rube, and then stammered out some kind of acceptance when he'd offered to come look at it. So now he was coming here to my shabby rented apartment, and no amount of frantic homemaking would make it look homey or presentable.

But surely he wouldn't judge me if he lived in one of the furnished apartment rentals too? Maybe we had the same drab couch and rickety coffee tables. We could laugh together about the vintage radiators with so many coats of paint that it obscured the filigree underneath, and the cabinet doors that all hung a little crooked. I tried to comfort myself with thoughts of Alistair washing his dishes at a twin version of my beat-up sink, but I just couldn't picture the intimidating mothman doing such a domestic task.

It probably didn't help my nerves that I could swear the little mushrooms were glaring at me. I was almost surprised when I came home last night to find that the frog wasn't sitting in his normal spot waiting for me, because it had happened that way so many times lately. How does a four-inch-long frog beat you home from where you released it outside? I don't know!

And then this morning, still no frog. That was a great success in my book. I finally had a frog-free home. But somehow, *somehow*, I got the vibe that these little low-fae were unhappy about this development. Perturbed, even. I'd think they'd be glad to not have to share their tiny pot with another creature, so I didn't understand the odd sense of annoyance that was emanating in waves from the low-fae. I was probably imagining things again though.

A knock at the door jerked me out of my musings, and I glanced out the window to see that dusk had fallen across the fog-coated streets below. "I can come by tomorrow evening and take a look at your tree," the mothman had offered yesterday, before I'd listened in horror as my mouth accepted his offer without my brain's permission. I tiptoed to the door and looked out the peephole to find... a wall of indistinct gray. I took a deep breath, pasted on a smile, and jerked the door open, only to have to step back because he was right there. I practically had a face full of fluff because he was hunched over awkwardly in my doorway, looking bleary-eyed and rumpled. His antennae were going in wonky directions and his mane fuzz stuck out in clumps every which way. He gripped the door frame with one hand and his other three arms dangled limply at his sides.

"Did you get into a fight?" I asked him. His mussed appearance did nothing to take the edge off of the menacing aura his stature and build presented.

Alistair lifted a hand to one eye and rubbed at it with a slow smile, a soft chirp sounding in his chest. "I just woke up," he buzzed. "I didn't know what time you went to sleep, and

I didn't want to be rude by making you wait." A big yawn stretched his jaw, revealing his teeny, tiny fangs and long, curled tongue. As he clicked his teeth shut, his antennae went haywire, jittering rapidly on his head and bouncing around until he was forced to slap his hands down on top of them, flattening the boisterous appendages against his skull. He hunched in place, looking as though the ceiling was raining down on top of him. "Sorry," he grumbled, his eyes squinting with annoyance.

"Sorry?" I wasn't sure exactly what he was apologizing for. His wayward antennae? Just waking up? His mussed appearance? My hands itched to smooth his fluff into place for him, and I wondered what it would feel like between my fingers. I blinked up at him and stepped back to allow him to come in if he wanted. "I'll be up for a while still, if you want to sleep for a little bit longer," I offered. "Have you had—" Breakfast? Dinner? What did nocturnal people call their first meal? I finally settled on, "—food?" I didn't even know what mothpeople ate. Perhaps I could offer him some... water?

He stepped through the door slowly, having to duck to fit his enormous height under the frame. Once he was through, he hesitantly lifted his hands from his head as if he expected his antennae to fritz out again immediately. They did not, instead laying plastered against his scalp in a mangled-looking mess of feathery fluff. He still kept two hands raised, just in case, while looking rather hunted. "Sorry," he repeated before relaxing and straightening to his full height. "No, I prefer not to ingest anything this early. Thank you very much, though. I'll have some fruit once I'm more awake." His gaze locked on my apple tree, and he made his way across the room, never glancing at my shabby couch or my throw blankets or even toward my kitchen. He only had eyes for my tree. "The others are not here?" he asked, sounding concerned.

"They're at the retail store," I explained.

He nodded absently and rumbled quietly, "I'd like to check it out sometime." A kindness, surely. But he turned to me, as if waiting for a response.

"Sure," I responded, not understanding what he wanted—did he feel as if he needed permission to visit my store?—but he nodded as if pleased. He then bent to inspect every leaf and limb, turning them up so he could see the undersides and then poking his fingers into the soil. It was fascinating to watch him move, the way the muscles in his shoulders bunched and the iridescent sheen on his wings as they caught the light.

"And what are you doing here?" he asked the mushrooms, clearly not expecting a reply. "Did you get tired of Miela's rough handling at the orchard? I've never understood how that child is exempt from your retaliations. Some warriors you are," he grumbled quietly.

My eyebrows crept upward. *Warrior mushrooms?*

"It needs more light," he said a bit louder, startling me out of my imaginings of tiny mushrooms holding even tinier wooden swords.

"This is the best window in the apartment!" I protested. I had a balcony at my condo in New Caelora, and I'd assumed the tree would be fine for the few months it took before I could move it back home. "And it's doing much better than it was before the mushrooms started growing."

Alistair turned to look at me, and his antennae perked up. "Is that so?"

I bit my lips—hard—to keep from smiling. His antennae were still a complete mess, bent in weird directions with the feathery tufts sticking out all higgledy-piggledy. I could feel my eyes shining with amusement though, and surely he could have spotted it from across the room.

"I would have you know that I'm refraining from shaking my coat out like a long-furred canine to spare your lovely apartment from a generous coating of 'mothman glitter,' as one friend generously describes my wing scales," he said primly, gesturing at the wings on his back. "You may thank me for my self-restraint at any time."

I couldn't tell if he was joking or not, so I said, "Thank you," although it sounded like a question as I said it.

"You're welcome," he said loftily, though I caught a hint of mirth that made me grin. How did he manage to be scary and cute at the same time? "You might consider moving your tree to my roof," he suggested quickly. "I would be happy to care for it along with my other plants, and you can come visit it or take it home whenever you like."

I blinked at him, trying to make sense of his suggestion. "Your... roof?"

He reached up to straighten one of his antennae and cleared his throat, almost as if he were nervous. "Yes. I keep all of my personal plants that need full sun on the roof here. The low-fae will have to relocate though; they don't do well in full sun." His other antenna needed a great deal more work, requiring three of his hands to untangle some of the wispy filaments.

"Oh, um, sure. I guess? You don't need the management's permission to go up there?" I started toward my tree, but he waved me away, hefting the cement pot easily with one arm in a way that made my cheeks feel hot for some reason. Even completely empty, I hadn't been able to lift that pot on my own—I'd rolled it to its place by the window.

"Come, I will show you," he declared. Tiny clouds of shimmering dust billowed off of him as he opened the door with his extra hands and snapped his wings together to pass through, grumbling at the mushrooms all the while as they hitched a ride. His wings looked curiously like a heavy cloak from behind.

I held back a bemused smile as he left a trail of his glitter down the hallway and up the back stairs, though why that amused me or why I even noticed, I couldn't say. I followed him into the fourth-floor hallway and—never having been to this floor before—was surprised to find it was a much shorter hallway with only two doors.

He opened one and held it for me like a gentleman, and I nearly gasped as I stepped inside.

His apartment was huge—a penthouse—with elaborate vintage molding around beautifully restored windows. The walls were a deep forest green with blue undertones, with the soft, subtle texture of hand-troweled clay pigments. Brass sconces cast a warm, amber glow that mingled with the muted, layered lighting of multiple lamps and strands of twinkle lights. An oversized, low-backed, tan leather couch sat behind a coffee table that looked to have been an antique wooden crate. It was moody, and masculine, and deliciously cozy. The subtle, musky scent of him was everywhere, and I inhaled deeply, trying to imprint it on my lungs.

"This is beautiful," I told him breathlessly as he brushed past me, carrying the tree toward the far wall where a large shelving system of iron pipes and stained wood was completely covered with trailing plants. "How did you convince the landlords to let you do all of this?"

Ancient looking wooden beams stretched across the ceiling, drawing my gaze across the large space to an open kitchen. I couldn't see much in the dim lamplight of the apartment, except for polished cement counter tops and some copper pots gleaming in the moonlight, which found its way in through several large skylights. It had so much *character.*

Alistair gave a low, buzzing laugh as he set my pot down near the shelves and turned to walk over to the kitchen. He pulled out a drawer and dug around before returning with a metal spatula. "I gave him a kiss and a wink and told him he was handsome." His fangs showed as his mouth pulled into a wide grin, and he gave a low chirp. "I'm teasing. I own this outright. The building was originally all condos, but an investor came in and bought up a bunch of the units to turn into student or apartment housing." He gave a small shrug and lifted a potted pothos off of his shelf.

I drifted toward the couch to watch what he was doing, reaching out unthinkingly to touch a soft, chunky-knit blanket that was piled on one end. The fibers were soft and dense, and my fingers came away covered in iridescent glitter.

The big mothman set the pothos next to my potted tree on the floor and tilted the tree toward it. He used the spatula to prod the low-fae out of their pot and into the pothos. "Oh, they're gonna be quite angry about this," he grumbled. "Ack! Oh, dear. So sorry!" he squawked as one of the littlest mushrooms tumbled out of the pot and onto the floor. "So very sorry!" Alistair repeated as he carefully slid his metal spatula under the mushroom and lifted it back to the pot, gently situating it in the new pot before addressing the rest of the fungal group. "Now, listen, you lot don't have to go home, but you can't stay here in this tree pot. It's going up on the roof and it'll be too sunny for you. You'll bake! But you're welcome to use this little pot in the meantime," he reassured them. After he got them moved, he handed me the pothos-mushroom pot—a ceramic pot with a pretty blue and bronze glaze. "This is yours now," he informed me. "Because you don't have any plants left in your apartment now, and every home needs a plant."

I took the pot, feeling strangely touched, and peered down at the little toadstools. They were all hunkered down in the soil now, with their faces hidden. Sure, I still had the plants at the store, but that wasn't the same as a plant in your house to make your heart happy for the sake of it.

"To the roof," Alistair instructed, easily hefting the tree pot again and leading the way to a metal door located in the wall behind the kitchen. He pushed it open and led me out into the night on a black metal stairwell connected to the side of the building, giving me a rueful grin that made my heart hammer in my chest as he paused to stick a doorstop under the door. "It locks when it closes, and then I'd have to fly you down, which I don't think you'd be too pleased about," he informed me with a chuckling buzz.

I felt my neck heat with both the embarrassing memory of being too scared to climb down from the tree yesterday and the unexpected image of how it might feel to be held tightly by all four of Alistair's muscular arms. *What has gotten into me??*

He was still chuckling to himself as we climbed the last of the stairs and stepped onto the rooftop. I stood, clutching my little pot of pothos vines, and stared. The entire space was covered in rows upon rows of potted sapling trees and flowering shrubs. There was an iron arbor supporting a stout vine covered in blooms that dripped with nectar. The scent that hung heavy in the air was intoxicating.

"Oh, Alistair," I breathed, completely at a loss for words. As I looked around, I realized nearly all the blossoms were white, the perfect shade to reflect the moonlight in what had to be a purposefully planned little moon garden. Long, silvery grasses rustled in the slight breeze, and I spotted a rare night-blooming sorenvine. Fireflies blinked their lights slowly in the distance.

Alistair gave a cheery buzz, his head pulling back slightly into his fluff but obviously pleased that I appreciated his little moon-lit sanctuary. This was clearly his happy place. "You like it?" he asked.

"I love it." I couldn't stop gazing at all the various elements.

The noise he made was very nearly a purr, and he practically hugged the apple tree pot to his chest. "I'm so glad. You're welcome to join me up here any time," he told me with a shy note to his voice. He stared at me for a short beat before seeming to shake himself free. "Come, let's put your tree over here where it will get the most light." He led me to a corner of the roof that was mostly dominated by glistening succulents and sun-loving wildflowers, where he tucked the pot next to the outer wall, chattering all the while about the sun's path of travel and proper airflow. After fussing with it for a moment and ultimately deciding he was satisfied with its placement, he drifted here and there to tell me about his favorite of the different details he'd incorporated—his favorite plants and the decorative elements he'd worked in.

Eventually, we sat in silence on a bench near the center of the space and simply breathed in the heady perfume of the surrounding flowers, content to watch the fireflies and the leaves that rustled in the breeze.

I was in heaven.

Chapter 5

Lilith

THE LITTLE POT OF vines felt like it had always existed on the side table next to my living room window. The toadstools eventually settled into their new home, though I suspected they preferred the apple tree to the pothos. Alistair assured me they would leave if they were terribly unhappy, but I had no idea how. *Mushrooms* could just up and leave my locked apartment? But he'd sounded completely sure of himself. My apartment remained frog-free as the days went by, so perhaps my upstairs neighbor had finally been the solution to that unusual problem.

I thought of the mothman strangely often as I went about the next few days, thinking back to the deep vibrating rumble of his voice as he talked me down out of the ibec tree or the careful way he phrased his suggestions so as not to come across too pushy or harsh. The soft clicks he made as he thought about his answers and the way his antennae seemed to have a mind of their own. His personality was as unique as his appearance, at least to me, since I'd never met anyone like him before. I wondered what he did for fun, other than gardening, and what kind of community he had grown up in. The more my thoughts lingered on him, the more my appreciation for his uniqueness grew.

Sometimes, when I heard the scratch of his talons start up at night, I'd consider inviting him down for evening tea. Then I'd remember that he'd said he didn't like to eat that early, so I'd drink my evening tea alone and go to bed. I'd even considered taking him some cookies as a way to thank him for taking care of my tree, but I didn't know if he even ate cookies, and in the end, I chickened out. He'd said I could come visit my tree any time I wanted and had seemed rather enamored at my reaction to his rooftop garden, but I didn't know how to approach him about it in a way that wouldn't seem like I didn't trust his skills as a horticulturist. *Hello, Alistair, I would like to check on the health of the tree you so generously offered to maintain for me.* That would just be awkward.

I found myself looking for him at the corner market when I shopped—surely he would shop there too, since it was the closest market—and was suddenly acutely aware of everyone's comings and goings at the apartment, but I never saw him. I even went back to the orchard one afternoon to buy a box of apples—it wasn't *stalking*; I'd wanted one anyway!—but he wasn't there. Our schedules must have been too disparate, or maybe he simply didn't want to be seen. The thought caused an odd pang in my chest and made me wonder what I was doing, so I decided to push him from my mind and refocus on the plant shop. Making friends here would just be a distraction anyway.

But then, one evening, there was a knock at my door, so timid and light I might have missed it if I hadn't been lost in my own head. I blinked at the mushrooms, and they blinked back at me, obviously having no answer for me about who might be calling, so I hauled myself off the couch to answer the door. A wall of gray greeted me through the peephole. Alistair stood looming in my doorway again, this time with his fluff in perfect order and his delicate antennae gracefully arching above his head. They only gave a tiny twitch this time before he gained control of them. He cleared his throat and hitched his fluff higher around his head, making me realize I'd been staring at his antennae. My face heated.

"Hello," he said before I recovered enough to greet him politely. His fingers were steepled between each opposing hand. "I was wondering if perhaps you might like to come over—if it's not too late, I mean—and visit your tree this evening. But if it is too late, then I completely understand and I apologize for bothering you!"

My mouth quirked at his invitation. *Visit my tree? How cute is that? And why hadn't I thought of that excuse?*

He kept going before I could respond. "Or we could discuss plants. Or if tonight isn't a good time, we could obviously reschedule for another evening. I just thought that since you hadn't been by to see your tree, maybe you would like to see how it's doing." His taloned fingers began to twist around each other as he gave a nervous sounding click.

A smile spread across my face. "I would love to come over and visit my tree."

He stood, staring at me owlishly, as if he were too surprised to respond.

"Would you like for me to bring up some tea for us to drink while we discuss plants?" I asked.

He gave an interested buzz, and his eyes brightened. "What kind of tea?"

And so, what started out as innocent tree-visiting and plant discussions quickly became fruit salad making—while he enumerated the various ways to determine which strawberries were at perfect ripeness and ranted about how honeydew melon was the worst fruit in existence—and spur of the moment jaunts to the smoothie stand in the student district. Then there were rooftop garden parties which consisted of actual gardening, not just sitting around eating cake *in* a garden, although that happened occasionally too, as long as the cake had fruit in it. Moon Blush apples randomly appeared in crates on my welcome mat, and Alistair started stopping by the plant shop just before closing.

He'd been hesitant to visit at first, even though he seemed to want to, but he finally came to see our new set up and even ended up chatting with Artem about various splicing methods. The old dryad didn't seem to know what to make of my talkative neighbor and all of his ideas about various ways to cobble trees together to build the *best* tree. I laughed every time I thought about my employee's baffled expressions at some of Alistair's suggestions, but I'd been so impressed at the way Alistair managed to pull Artem out of his proverbial shell. They had been like wary cats when he first walked in, each unsure of the other with nothing more than a prickly greeting and a quintessential man-nod. But Alistair's enthusiastic excitement as he exclaimed to me over every tiny plant baby in the store had quickly won over the old man, who tip-toed closer to hear the mothman's words of praise about how healthy this one looked or what an adorable leaf structure that one possessed. It wasn't long before Artem was discussing the finer points of mycorrhizal inoculation in homemade potting soil and the preferred PH of stone fruits.

But Alistair's original reticence to visit the shop, even though he had expressed interest in doing so, stuck with me as I found myself thinking of him more and more these days. It was almost as if he had seemed unsure of his welcome in the store, though I'd invited him half a dozen times before he finally showed up. When I asked Alistair about his hesitancy, he just shrugged and changed the subject. I finally managed to pin down Artem one morning while he was watering plants. Not literally, obviously. The man was as big as a tree. I didn't want to put him on the spot, so I mentioned my curiosity in the most off-hand way I could, and I *might* have set down a steaming hot cup of his favorite honey-flavored brew that I'd picked up for him on my way in. I could tell he wanted to be his usual grumpy, tight-lipped self as he eyed my proffered bribe, but he slowly reached out to take it and took a long sip while giving me an unimpressed look, before finally giving me a crumb of information.

"The previous owners were pretty opinionated about, well, everything, I guess," he said, smacking his lips and giving his own little shrug.

I frowned at him, trying to decipher that, and decided to press him a little harder. "About Alistair?" I asked, wondering if something had happened between him and the previous owners, but half expecting Artem not to answer. He could be cagey at the best of times, and I was just waiting for him to get that shifty look in his deep mahogany eyes before he clammed up and sidled off to go sweep the cobwebs out of a back corner—coffee bribe in tow.

But he surprised me. "Hm, they thought the university and all of its research into new plants was snooty and high-minded," Artem clarified in his low rumble, scratching lightly at the bark on his left cheek before taking another swig of coffee.

My frown deepened, remembering how Artem had once told me that the previous owners didn't want to work with the "head researcher" at the university because he was "persnickety," but one of his first pieces of advice to me was to go order some of the new trees at the university, so obviously *he* hadn't felt that way about the research.

"They didn't like him?" I guessed aloud, and I knew by the way Artem half-cringed that I'd guessed correctly. I could just picture sweet, excitable Alistair feeling unwelcome at the largest, most established plant nursery in the region and how that must have hurt his feelings. I thought of his wall of plants at home and the rooftop garden he so lovingly tended.

"I like him well enough," Artem said grumpily, interrupting my thoughts, before finishing off his coffee and picking up the watering wand to continue his morning chores.

My smile was small but genuine. "I like him too," I said, touched.

One day, several months later, a new yoga studio opened up a few blocks from our building. New Caelora had been peppered with tiny boutique yoga studios, usually frequented by flocks of fashionable upper-crust elves who all wanted to be part of the trendy new exercise regimen from the human world. I'd always wanted to try it, but since my friends were more the 'mimosas and brunch' sort, I'd never had anyone to go with me.

"Would you be interested in joining me?" I asked Alistair tentatively that Friday evening as he sat across from me on my threadbare couch. I could go by myself, but the thought of walking in alone to try something brand new with a group of complete strangers left an uneasy feeling in the pit of my stomach. I probably wouldn't go alone.

"Yoga?" He paused briefly in his task of putting away the last of our board game pieces before hurriedly shoving the rest of them into his bag with a delighted sounding click. "I would love to try that!" he said. "I own several pieces of exercising apparel that would be perfect," he informed me, "and would be delighted to join you." His eagerness was palpable as we finished our tea and decided to attend the very next day.

Now, Alistair was often excitable, but I hadn't been prepared for just *how* excited he was to wear his "exercising apparel." I opened the door to his knock the next morning at o'dark-thirty to find he was still bright-eyed and chipper from the night before. He was wearing a loose-fitting white muscle shirt with the neck stretched wide enough to fit his expansive mane. Bold, black letters declared, 'I [HEART] LAMP,' with a bright red heart design in the middle. I'd never seen him wear clothing before. He was very enthusiastic about it.

"My friend Sidney brings me the *best* shirts from the Void," he said with a happy chirp, referencing the human world where most of us never ventured. "This one is rather comfortable, I must say, and I *do* love lamps!"

My grin was permanently etched on my face the whole way to the studio as I trotted along beside him, peppering him with questions about his clothing. Why did he wear a shirt, but no pants? And if he was so thrilled about them, why didn't he wear them more often?

"Mothpeople don't wear clothes!" he said, like it should be obvious. "They just get in the way when we fly, and it's hard to make them fit with our wings and they usually tug and pull on my fluff," he said, carding his fingers through the tuft of gray fuzz sticking out the stretched neck hole of his shirt.

My smile grew impossibly wider.

"But," he continued, "since my friend Sid bought me this one, it's special. And it's more comfortable than most clothes. I'm not big on exercise for sport, so now I get a chance to wear it!"

I felt my eyes crinkle at the corners as I failed to contain my mirth. "I don't see how trousers would interfere with your flying."

He gave me a haughty look that made a laugh burst out of me like a short bark. "Have you seen how my legs are built?" he asked, gesturing at the giant hocks that bent oddly halfway down his legs and the large, sprawling talons he walked on. "I don't even know how I'd get them on," he declared as we entered the studio and approached the reception desk. But he wasn't finished, disregarding the fact that a stranger now stood in front of us as he continued his diatribe with his non-existent nose in the air. "And it's not like we need them for modesty's sake. All our bits are on the inside, as they should be."

The receptionist—a stoutly built bridge-troll with graphite colored skin and a cute pixie cut—went wide-eyed at that comment, causing me to dissolve into a fit of giggles as I apologized to her on his behalf, signed us in, and dragged him off to pick up our rented yoga mats.

The classroom smelled of stale sweat and cleaning solution, but not overpoweringly so, and the instructor, a cheerful, energetic elvish girl, greeted us with curious eyes as we entered the space. Bright light streamed in through two large windows off to the side and some kind of ancient lyre music filtered in from a back room. The space was small, but so was the group—a mixture of what looked to be mostly college-age kids and a few older locals. A goblin, a shifter, an orc, and several more elves made up the group, and none of them seemed to bat an eye at my mothman companion. We looked for a place to set up our mats, but there wasn't much room left. "Here," he told me, "you take this spot in front, so you can see."

I ignored his offer and began to unroll my mat behind him. "I don't want to be that close," I whispered, not wanting to look like a fool in front of the instructor.

He groused at me that he was too big to be able to see around and I wouldn't be able to follow the instructor, but I stubbornly hid behind him until he gave up when our teacher began to talk, the peppy young elf introducing herself as Brianna and explaining how the class would go. She talked about body awareness and mindfulness, and Alistair was right—I couldn't see very much of her—but that was okay, because I could just watch him and follow his lead. And then I realized as she started with a series of gentle opening stretches that I actually had the best view in the whole room. Because Alistair's booty was *right* there in front of me.

I'd always noticed Alistair was well-built. It would be impossible not to; he was huge. But what I hadn't noticed—due to his large wings, which he usually kept pulled tight against his back—was that the man's posterior was *fine*. I caught myself wondering multiple times whether it stuck out far enough to balance a cupcake on it. How did a man with an exoskeleton have what appeared to be such shapely looking glutes? It made no sense.

I really did try my best to focus on participating in class, to follow his movements as he followed the instructor. But it was hard with Alistair parked right there in front of me the whole time. How was he so good at this? He was surprisingly adept for someone who claimed to never exercise and had never tried yoga before. He had muscles where muscles should not be. I also never exercised, and my body could only be described as softly rounded. Maybe a little plump, even. I tottered and struggled to form the correct shapes with my body, but his poses flowed easily from one to the next as Brianna calmly gave her placid instructions to the room.

Motes of scales drifted from Alistair as we changed positions, carrying his scent with them as they settled onto me, and something about that scent *affected* me. I was already hot, but the warm, musky scent of his scales made its own heat twist low in my belly, my thoughts turning fuzzy, and my heart pounding more than was called for by this situation. The slow, warm curl of desire pulsing and tightening deep within me was a heady distraction until he quickly darted a hand out to save me when I nearly face planted onto my mat while trying the Standing Forward Bend. "Careful, darling," he murmured as he righted me.

It took me a second to make sense of his words.

Darling.

He'd called me *darling*.

Yoga with Alistair became a weekly Saturday ritual, and it never failed to amaze me how many different ways the muscular mothman could contort his multitude of limbs. I always took the spot behind him so I could continue to watch his well-rounded glutes flex and his biceps bulge, and thankfully he never caught on that I wasn't just hiding from the instructor. It usually ended up with me laughing into my yoga mat while Alistair tried to untangle me from myself, complaining all the while about how I managed to mess the poses up so badly when

I had so few limbs, but I loved it. I loved the sound of his laugh and the luxurious scent of him and the way he spoke and all of his little mannerisms and gestures. I looked forward to every planned encounter and found myself thinking about him constantly. I was in major crush territory, and I didn't even know how it had happened. It had been weeks since I'd even thought about New Caelora.

One evening we ventured to the rooftop, mugs of my favorite peach-flavored tea in hand, and he made a frustrated sound when the door clicked shut. "It locked us out," he announced with a sigh.

I took a deep breath and set my tea down on his potting bench. This was an inevitable eventuality with a door like that, and I refused to allow myself to panic.

"It's okay. I can do this." The thought of him flying me down from the roof of the fourth floor was terrifying, but I knew I could trust him. "Please don't drop me," I said anyway, my voice shaking as I squeezed my eyes shut, readying myself for him to pluck me from the ground.

But he chuckled and said, "No, darling. I will go down and prop the door open again." He was still laughing to himself as he launched into the sky and gracefully dropped toward the ground below, his massive wings thrumming powerfully.

I loved it when he called me darling.

I. Was. So. Smitten.

"HAVE YOU EVER TRIED the fuzz berry pastries?" Alistair asked me early one morning as we stood in front of the doughnut case at a little hole-in-the-wall cafe. I'd never been to this one, usually opting for the chain coffee shop on the way to work that the university students favored, but Alistair told me this one was a local institution. I'd woken up a bit early to be able to meet him here for breakfast before opening the nursery, since he'd just finished his work at the lab.

"I don't think I've ever heard of fuzz berries," I admitted. "Is that a real fruit?"

He puffed up with excitement. "Oh, yes!" he told me before turning to the barista. "Two fuzz berry pastries, please. On my tab," he said, taking the puffy-looking confections carefully once the young naga removed them from the case, plated them, and handed them over.

"I can pay for my own breakfast," I said as he led me to a little table by the window covered with a red and white checkered cloth. It looked like it might have been older than I was, the white squares yellowed with age and worn from heavy use. Alistair knew I loved to people-watch, and he always seemed to find some strange amusement from watching me as I watched the people. This cafe was a little off the beaten path, so the street was nearly empty except for a slow trickle of people stepping in to buy something from the counter before hustling out again.

"Hush," he said, waving me off as he set one of the plated pastries in front of my chair. "What if you don't like it? It's a bit of an acquired taste," he told me, "but it's one of my favorites."

"High praise, coming from you. What do you like about it?" I inquired, latching on to the opportunity to learn something new about him. His insights about food were always unexpected, and there was something about the pleasure he found in simple fruits that always made me smile.

"Oh, I love the flavor, of course," he said with a happy buzz as he used his long talon-like claws to tease apart the crisp, crackled surface of the dough. "It's very tart, be warned." He popped a bit of the fruit filling into his mouth, bypassing the outer pastry crust all together, and gave a deeper, more rumbling buzz. "But mostly it reminds me of my childhood."

Butterflies had threatened to overwhelm me at the sound of his pleasant, purr-like rumbling, so I'd focused on watching a little harpy child toddle down the sidewalk toward the cafe entrance with her mother, only briefly glancing at Alistair as he spoke, but now my gaze was riveted to the way his antennae twitched and his eyes warmed as he enjoyed his treat. "Tell me more," I encouraged, feeling a smile threaten. The man could talk for hours about tree genomes and the best methods for breaking bud dormancy, but talking about himself seemed like a foreign concept.

"I grew up picking fuzz berries in the woods behind my house," he said with a little shrug. "The bushes aren't exactly rare, per se, at least not where I'm from, but the berries are quite delicate. They don't keep, so you won't find them in stores."

I considered this as I took my first bite, enjoying the way the sweetened outer bun buffered the intense tartness of the berry. "Oh! That's very good," I told him sincerely. "That's dangerously good."

"It is, isn't it?" he agreed. "I've never found any other shops that sell baked goods that use them. We'd spend every day during the summer searching for them, me and my best friend. Rampaged around in the woods like little berry-juice smeared primitives. And the flowers!" he exclaimed. "They only open at night, and they have the most delicious nectar. You can't imagine the scent."

"Hmm," I murmured, enjoying the taste. "Do you miss them? Why don't you grow them?" I wondered aloud, thinking of his big rooftop garden. Surely, if anyone could grow them, he could.

"Oh, all the time. I tried to grow them several times, actually, but they're very specifically adapted to the region where they're from. There's not enough humidity here, and the nights just don't get cold enough. They can't have too much light, but they still need enough for their berries to ripen. It's a whole ordeal," he sighed. "These little pastries capture the base flavor, but all the nuance is gone."

I frowned at my half-eaten sweet, noting the dark purple-blue compote and trying to imagine the way it tasted when it was fresh, but I couldn't. "That's sad."

He smiled at me—a small secretive smile that hid something I didn't understand. "It is, a little. I do miss the flavor, but I can still taste them whenever I go home."

"Do you go home often?" I asked, already knowing the answer.

"No, not often," he said, confirming my hunch. "And even if I did, it would be quite a trial lining up my trip to match with their very short fruiting season," he said, his smile rueful this time. "But, I think, somehow, that fleeting window of availability, their rarity, their uniqueness... It all makes them that much more special."

I pondered this, my gaze resting on the way his hands skillfully dissected the baked good so that only the barest sliver sullied the berry filling as a vessel for carrying it to his mouth without dirtying his talons. How many delicious fruits would I never know because I only ate what was available in grocery stores?

"What kinds of things did you do in New Caelora when you were growing up?" Alistair asked conversationally. "What are you missing here that you loved back home?" There was an odd light in his eyes as he asked, as if he were afraid to know the answer.

Everything.

As soon as the thought popped into my mind, I knew it wasn't entirely true.

Chapter 6

Lilith

THE THICK, HANDMADE PAPER of the wedding invitation was rough against my fingers as I followed the looping scrawl of gold foiled letters with my eyes for the hundredth time. When I'd received the missive from an old college friend shortly after moving here, I'd been so focused on being miserable and getting the shop up and running that I hadn't had room to be excited about the prospect of returning home to New Caelora for only a few short days. Obviously, I loved my home and wanted to be back there, but the exhaustion of the recent move and upending my life had burned out any desire to travel anytime soon, especially for something as short as a weekend. So I'd begrudgingly sent my RSVP, arranged for a friend to attend as my plus-one, stuck the note on my fridge, and put it out of my mind while I dealt with rearranging my life and revitalizing the new business.

Eventually, after having rested and settled in, I'd found myself feeling more positive about the trip, even as short as it was. The pretty, hand-pressed paper full of flower petals and little bits of colored paper would catch my eye from where it had hung on my freezer for the last few months, slowly becoming something fun and familiar to look forward to amongst the annoyances of learning a new and unfamiliar place. It was only recently, within the last few weeks even, that I began to look at the invitation with a hint of dread again, although for an entirely different reason. Sure, getting to see my friends and grab a bite at my favorite cafe and sleep in my own bed and drop in on my parents would be lovely, no doubt. *And yet...*

I couldn't help the way my mind constantly drifted back to my thoughtful, funny, shy, excitable, handsome, adorable upstairs neighbor. This would be the first weekend in months that we weren't going to be attending yoga together on Saturday morning or having tea on Friday night. He'd reacted to the news that I would be away for a few days by loading me down with a bag of his precious apples and some fuzz berry pastries for the trip home. “You might get hungry,” he’d insisted as he folded them into my hands before I left for the train, as if I couldn’t purchase food myself on that very same train. “But you can’t buy *these* on your train,“ he said with a grumpy buzz when I voiced the amused thought, his antennae twitching as he fussed over me. “What if you waste away to nothing while you’re gone? That’s not going to happen on my watch,” he said with a put-upon air.

I’d rolled my eyes with a smile, explaining that my plump derriere wouldn’t allow me to waste away in a matter of a few days, even in the extremely unlikely situation of being unable to find food.

“Well, I wouldn’t allow it,” he’d said haughtily, as if such a thing were even a legitimate concern, and I’d chuckled at him, wishing not for the first time that *he’d* been the plus-one I’d invited to the wedding. I consoled myself that I had a hard time picturing him in the concrete and glass confines of the city. Even our parks were neat and tidy, perfectly manicured gardens without a hint of the wildness that the forest races often preferred. Alistair had his orchard rows, but even they seemed somehow different from the exacting order that elves practiced in our cities.

But I had already secured a longtime friend from my girl's school days as my plus-one, long before I'd actually become friends with Alistair. Merri was another elvish girl I'd grown up with, from a similar working-class family as my own. She also knew Stella, the bride, from college and had recently moved back to New Caelora herself with her husband and son. I figured it would be a good way to introduce her around and help her make some new friends, and I couldn't wait to see her again. It went without saying that I *so appreciated* her acting as a buffer for me at the wedding, in case our other college friends weren't able to attend. I didn't normally mind small talk as long as it had some kind of purpose—like discussing what kind of plants a person liked as I helped them figure out what to purchase at the nursery, or talking about preferred train routes with one of my old neighbors who traveled to the same parts of the city as me—but the aimless, time-killing chatter with complete strangers at something like a wedding was utterly dreadful. Knowing I had an old friend to come with me made me more comfortable.

As busy as we'd both been, me with the move and my friend, Stella, with planning her wedding, I hadn't been able to chat with her and find out who from our college friend group was attending. At least this way, by bringing along someone who would already know our friend group, I would be able to concentrate on them and be present with them in a way I hadn't been able to in years. At least, that's what I told myself.

When I stepped off the train in New Caelora that evening, I was greeted by the familiar scent of cleansing rain that so often showered the city, cooking food, and waste bins in desperate need of being emptied in the hustle and hubbub of the busy station. Dodging the many passersby both inside the station and on the sidewalk out front was a dance I'd known all my life, but I wasn't sure I'd ever taken notice of just how *many* people there were before. After hours of traveling, all I wanted was to get home and crawl into bed, so I flagged down a passing cab and gladly paid the higher fare for one of the speedy wyvern-drawn carriages. The elvish driver never spoke to me, just a tilt of his head to acknowledge he was listening as I relayed my address and a nod of thanks when I paid him before getting out. It was lovely.

However, when I finally arrived at my downtown condo and began opening windows to freshen the musty air that had accumulated in my unused home, I discovered that the aforementioned cleansing rain that was so ubiquitous in my city had been coming in through a split in one of the window casings in my living room—and evidently had been for some time. Dripping water had saturated the wall below the window, the hardwood floor around it, and several pieces of furniture nearby. I was in the middle of frantically trying to sop up the puddles of water as I waited for the building super to arrive when Merri, my plus-one, sent me a spectral messenger. I answered immediately, pushing some of my magic into the little pebbles we referred to as calling stones, assuming Merri wanted to compare notes on what I was wearing tomorrow or double check the time I was picking her up, and I didn't want to put her off and then forget to respond while dealing with the mess in front of me.

"Oh, Lilith, I am *so sorry*, but I'm going to have to cancel for tomorrow," her voice said as the lines of rainbow-colored spirit danced and flickered in the space in front of me. Spectrals had been carrying our messages for us since time immemorial, feeding off the magic we pushed into our little chips of stone for them as payment for their services, but that wasn't what I was paying attention to just now. "Little Bartleby has been teething lately, and he's got a tiny bit of a fever just now, so I'll need to stay home with him tomorrow," she explained, referring to her one year-old-son with a woe-be-gone sigh.

I was stunned, not knowing how to respond. Far be it from me to know how to deal with a teething toddler, but Merri had a husband, who also happened to be her child's father, and she had planned for him to watch their baby during the wedding anyway. "I'm... sorry to hear that," I told her, my statement coming out sounding like a question. I didn't want to be presumptuous, but... "Is it not possible for your husband to stay with—"

"No, sorry," she cut me off, her mind already clearly made up. "Chadwick just isn't as good with him as I am," she said, referring to her husband. "And a baby really just needs his mommy, you know? You understand."

A lump formed in my throat. "Sure," I lied.

"I'd love to get together after the wedding though," she inserted hastily. "Maybe the day after, if you're still here?"

"I'll be here," I said numbly, not understanding how she could know her baby would be well enough to be without her the day after tomorrow if he wasn't well enough for tomorrow. I'd planned to stay through Monday so I could stop in to see my uncle at the shop and visit my parents, but I could rearrange my plans on Sunday if I needed to make sure there was time for her too. None of my other friends had been able to meet up this weekend, so I'd kept my trip short. Just long enough to attend the wedding and see my family.

"Great! Talk soon," she said before the spectral winked out, leaving me in my empty, stuffy apartment with a dripping window and no date to the wedding tomorrow.

"THIS IS UTTERLY DISTASTEFUL."

The elvish man next to me hadn't shut up about how much he hated the wedding since he'd taken his seat at my table after the ceremony. He was a dark elf, with gorgeous, flowing silver hair and an impeccably tailored suit. The permanent expression on his face looked like he'd just caught a whiff of old cat piss. His wife sighed from her seat beside him.

"No, *Darla*," he whispered aggressively, as if she'd actually spoken. "*It is.* You know his parents have to be completely disgusted. It's bad enough he's marrying a—" His eyes cut to the side, taking in the other couple seated with us at the table, and correcting the word he was going to say. "—a *non-elf*. But the least he could have done was provide them a dignified wedding. Something they wouldn't have to be ashamed of." He'd been about to say, "marrying a *goblin*," because my friend Stella, the bride, was just that—she was a cheerful little goblin with big doe eyes, impossibly cute freckles, and a wide, impish smile who'd lived on my floor in college. She'd met a seemingly nice elvish man who worked in finance with her after she graduated, and now they were getting married in a small garden wedding in the city. This asshole was talking about *my friend!*

His vitriol surprised me. Though New Caelora was one of the oldest Elvish cities, and certainly more homogenous than many other cities within our realm, it still had tons of diversity. Mixed race couples had been a non-issue for generations, and our generations were very long lived. I'd been somewhat shielded from the prejudices of the upper classes due to having grown up in a middle-class family, but I'd still not expected someone from our generation to feel the way he did, let alone be bold enough to say such a thing *out loud,* at the very couple's wedding, in front of their other goblin wedding guests.

"*Excuse* me—" I started to respond, outrage growing in my chest, but the goblin man across from us, who had clearly picked up the subtext of what Mr. Prissypants was putting down, forcefully interrupted me with a sneering, sarcastic, "Right, right. I was just saying the same thing to my wife too, you know? A traditional *goblin* celebration, right here in the middle of the city. I bet we could get a bonfire five stories tall going right here in this park." The goblin's wife swatted half-heartedly at his arm, rolling her eyes but ultimately choosing to focus on the buffet line, trying to see when it would be our table's turn to join the fray.

I cracked a smile at the smaller man's sarcasm. Where elves were known for our overly ritualistic, hours long wedding ceremonies that were often shows of wealth and stature, goblins traditionally hosted a raucous, roaring bonfire set deep in the woods. From the way Stella described it, everyone the couple and their extended families had ever known would be invited and the fire would be kept going for days as they roasted pigs and chestnuts and drank themselves silly. It sounded like a blast, and I kind of wished she'd opted for a traditional goblin wedding. At least people like this elvish asshole would have self-selected out of attending, but I understood why they'd opted for something tamer.

"I think it's incredibly charming that Stella and Ryne decided to do their own thing for their wedding," I told the asshole-elf sitting to my left, trying to deescalate the interaction when he sneered at the goblin man in return. The goblin man was more than a head shorter than the elf, but he was surprisingly muscular for a goblin, and I was already having visions of the smaller man with dark red skin and low-set, pointed ears climbing onto a chair to launch himself at the elf.

It had been a cute little wedding ceremony, followed by the guests gathering for a catered lunch at round white-clothed tables in a stepped down part of the garden nearby. A white cloth tent provided shade where the towering park trees were sparse, and birdsong and a string quartet provided background music. More and more of the younger generations were opting for these small, elegant, modern weddings they saw pictured in magazines or tabloids, and Stella and Ryne had chosen to go that route rather than hold to one family's traditional ceremonies and leave the other out. At least this way, both families were equally left out. And it was true that both sets of parents were probably not the happiest with their own people's traditions being eschewed, but to assume they were *ashamed*? That was a reach. And to criticize their marriage to one another while sitting at their wedding? Beyond the pale.

"It shows a complete lack of regard for their elders and everything they worked for," he continued, gazing around the decorated space and pointedly not making eye contact with the goblin man who was watching him with narrowed eyes. If any goblin could have kicked Mr. Prissypants' ass, I'd bet money on this one.

"I don't agree," I responded. "Tradition is something you can be guided by if that's something you want, but if those traditions no longer work for you, then they become an unasked-for burden rather than a gift. I think there's beauty in creating something unique with your new family." Why did we have to assign some kind of moral value to *the way things had always been*?

"Or perhaps they just come off looking like tacky, self-centered children," he retorted dryly, and the goblin man scoffed at him in return.

"Felis, you're embarrassing me," his wife whispered, finally giving a real name to the jerk as she seemed to shrink in on herself while looking down at her napkin wrapped silverware.

"This wedding is what's embarrassing."

The goblin decided he'd had enough, lifting his arm and jabbing a meaty finger at the table in front of him. "Why are you even h—"

"Look, Arek! It's food time!" The goblin's wife was up out of her chair in a heartbeat, tugging on his elbow. With a last irritated scowl for the very rude Felis, he clamped his lips together and allowed himself to be dragged toward the buffet line.

Seeing that the woman was right, I stood to follow them, leaving our elvish table mates to argue with one another about proper behavior at a wedding.

"That pretentious, weasel-faced prat..." Arek, the goblin man, grumbled when I joined the line behind them.

I nodded in silent agreement.

"Ignore them, dear ones," his wife said to both of us. "Your dress is beautiful, honey. I love the shimmer," she told me before she squeaked out an excited, "Oh, Arek, look! They've got roast pig puffs!"

I looked down at my dress and quickly realized that, though Alistair had never been around me when I'd worn this outfit, the shimmer she'd complimented was mothman dust. His sparkly scales had so thoroughly coated all of my things that nothing in my life could escape them. I felt a private smile spread across my face at the thought. I long ago stopped caring about the glittery coating that came away on my skin whenever I touched him. Every time I found the iridescent specks in my house or on my jacket, I couldn't help but smile to myself. They were a private reminder of the adorable, imposing, winged man who left them behind wherever he went.

"Do you like roast pig puffs too?" the goblin woman asked, misinterpreting my smile. She bore a lighter colored skin than her husband, a dusky pink color with the usual brighter pink coloration on her nose and ear tips that most goblins seemed to sport. Her eyes, like my friend Stella's, were a deep, soft brown. "I just love them with the bitter fern sauce," she continued. "They always hit the spot at weddings!"

"You'll have to show me how to eat one," I responded politely as I picked up my plate, and her eyes positively lit up with curiosity.

"You've never had one? Oh, you must try it. And the braised oyster mushrooms too," she added as she began to load down both of our plates, chattering about the different goblin foods all the while.

"Oh, now you've gone and gotten her started," her husband muttered good-naturedly.

Luckily, Felis was gone from the table when we returned, and neither he nor his wife reappeared while we ate. Arek's wife—Edis, she told me—talked animatedly all through dinner about the food and the wedding and how she was distantly related to Stella's family. I sat quietly, stuffing my face and making appropriate noises at appropriate intervals, and was grateful for both her good cheer and the fact that I didn't really need to contribute much to the conversation. Arek wasn't much of a talker either, so it seemed that she was used to running the show. I liked her immensely, but by the end of the evening, I was exhausted. It made me grateful for the comfortable silence that often existed between Alistair and me when we sat together while enjoying his rooftop garden. It made me wish—yet again—that he'd been the one I invited to the wedding as my guest. Although, I was glad he hadn't been exposed to the rude elf's remarks, and I guessed that he probably wouldn't have enjoyed the pig puffs as much as I did. I left as soon as was socially acceptable, stopping by the wedding party's table to make my goodbyes.

"Thank you so much for coming, Lilith," Stella said as I wrapped her in a hug. Her dress was a light pink organza confection that set off her pretty mauve colored complexion. She looked like the world's most adorable cupcake. "It really means a lot to me to have you here. I'm sorry more of our school friends didn't attend to keep you company. I hope the seating arrangement wasn't objectionable."

"Edis and Arek were wonderful," I told her, the only true thing I could say about the seating arrangement. "And the food was delicious. Thank you for allowing me to celebrate you and Ryne."

Since I had a little more time than I'd expected due to leaving the wedding early, I decided to stop by my parent's house afterwards. This way, my day wouldn't be so packed tomorrow if Merri still wanted to do something.

"Don't you worry about that leaky window," my dad said as we were finishing up our visit. "I'll make sure to stop by and check that your super has gotten it patched up nice and tight."

My mom took my empty cup of tea from my hands and went bustling off to the sink with it.

"Mom, I can do that myself," I called after her. "She doesn't need to clean up after me like I'm a guest," I told my dad as I collected my napkin. "It makes me feel like a stranger. And are you sure you have time to do that this week? Downtown is a little bit out of your way."

He waved me off and patted my shoulder. "I'll make time. And she's your mom, you know how she is."

"Do you want to take some of your plants home with you?" My mom popped back into the room, practically like a jack-in-the-box, carrying one of my leather ferns. "Surely you must miss them. Isn't your new place just utterly dull without them? Do you want to go through your old bedroom and see if there's anything you want to take? I can go get your bins. We can go through them right now."

It was nine o'clock at night. "No, not right now, Mom," I said with a groan. She'd been caring for my plants—which I appreciated—having moved them in among the dozens of her own plants. "I have plants, don't worry." The pothos that Alistair had given me was happy and thriving in my living room, and my apple tree was living its best life on his rooftop. I stood up to hug her. "And I don't want the bins. Please, just throw them out. Or donate them. Or I'll throw them away next time I come." I'd tried to get rid of it all before, but she was horrified at the thought of disposing of my childhood macaroni art and yellowed trophies or the old, mangled toys that I didn't even remember playing with. So now, every time I came over, she tried to get me to take them home with me. Going through the old bins was the last thing I wanted to do on a quick trip home to visit.

"No! That's your stuff! I can't toss out your stuff. What if your kids want it someday? I'll just keep it in your old closet until you want it."

I had never really wanted kids of my own, but for some reason, the first image that popped into my mind was of me trying to cram a caterbaby into one of my old jumpers with not enough armholes. I shook off the old thought and sighed before kissing her on the forehead. We would have this conversation for the rest of my life, I was sure. "I love you, Mom," I said as I gripped her tightly. "Thank you for taking care of my plants."

I was just so tired.

My stop by Blossom and Bonsai the next morning was quiet and uneventful. Melantha was doing a great job filling in for me, and

I brought her a cup of her favorite coffee as thanks. The stock boys were all new hires I didn't know, and it was weird not having a grumpy dryad drifting to-and-fro among the plants. My uncle was always pleased to see me, of course, but they were all busy getting the store ready to open and I didn't want to be a distraction. I air-kissed them both, checked to make sure the current financial records were satisfactory—they were—and headed back home to check in with Merri.

Once I was home, I pulled the locket containing the strand of Merri's hair from the string of leather that I kept them on and used it with a calling stone to summon a spectral messenger. The little spirits needed some kind of anchor—a little piece of the person you were sending them to—to be able to find their destination. Because of this, we couldn't call for just anyone; it had to be someone we were close enough to for them to gift you a piece of their person. It occurred to me that if Alistair had been capable of using the calling stones, I had enough of his 'glitter' in my clothes to be able to send him a message, with or without him purposefully giving me a piece of his fluff. Unfortunately, the older forest dwelling races, like mothmen and dryads, didn't have the type of magic used to power the little stones. I felt a little glum that I couldn't send him a quick message to ask if he'd gone to yoga without me or what the mushrooms were up to.

"Hello, Merri, I just wanted to see how your little one was doing and if you still wanted to try to get together before I leave tomorrow morning," I told the dancing wisps of light that spun in front of me as the little spectral collected my message for her.

Merri's response was immediate. "Hi, Lilith! Bartleby's doing great. So much better this morning. I hope the wedding went well. I wanted to see if you care to join us at The King's Ace for dinner this evening at seven!"

"Oh, uh." I stumbled over my response because I'd expected her to want to know more about the wedding since she hadn't been able to go, but I recovered quickly. "Sure, of course. I love King's Ace." But something about her wording was unexpected. "Who is 'us'? Is Chadwick coming?"

"Oh, no, he's going to be playing a game of paddle ball with his friends," she responded dismissively. "My upline told me to get some of my friends together this weekend to talk about a business opportunity with you, and she's going to be explaining how it all works to everyone. And I think you are just *so amazing*. I *immediately* thought of you when she asked and how you would be perfect for joining my business with me. How would you like to pick your own hours and work from home selling the hottest new weight loss shakes?"

I completely deflated. Here I'd thought I was getting together with an old friend to catch up with her about her moving back home to her old city and her new little family and recent marriage, but she was really just trying to rope me into some kind of multi-level marketing scheme. "Merri, do you even know what I do for a living?" I asked, my confusion and disappointment coloring my words, as it was rapidly becoming clear to me that she had no idea who I was these days and didn't actually care.

"Well, no." Her bravado faltered before she found it again, continuing with a false brightness. "But everyone is open to change. You could even do this in your spare time and keep your day job if you wanted!"

I closed my eyes and took a deep breath. It was probably pointless to argue with her, but my hurt feelings leaked through anyway. "So you have no idea what I do as a job, but you *immediately* thought I would be the perfect fit to join *your* business... selling weight loss shakes?"

"I run *my own* business selling *Skinny Slurp: The most delicious weight loss shakes!* And you would be running *your* own business, as my mentee! It doesn't really matter specifically what you're doing right now. It's about your personality, and how you're such a go-getter!" The false bravado was back in full force.

"Do you not hear yourself?" I asked her, completely baffled and unhappy. We'd been friends once, but it didn't seem like we were even compatible anymore. "Forget about dinner, Merri. I am absolutely not interested in any of that, so I'm going to pass on coming tonight. Please don't invite me to anything like this again." I cut off the supply of my magic to the calling chip that was pressed between my thumb and my forefinger, and the spectral messenger immediately winked out, flitting off to find the next message being offered for delivery.

I walked to my room, tossed what little clothes I'd brought into my bag, making up my mind to return to my little college town a day early, and then tossed one last scathing look at my leaking windowsill as I left my apartment. I was angry for many reasons: that my weekend home had been tainted by a bad friend, that nothing had been particularly pleasant, that *nothing* had felt like home. The whole time I had been here had been akin to trying to fit myself into a jacket that had shrunk in the wash. It looked the same, and seemed the same, but it just didn't fit me right anymore. The entire time I'd been here, I'd been thinking about Alistair and how my heart fluttered at his deep, buzzy voice and that *irritated* me too. He'd ruined my dislike of that shabby little village with his wing sparkles and his quiet questions. He'd made it seem more like home than my real home. I wasn't even sure which one was my real home anymore. And that made me angry too.

"To the train station, please," I told the cart driver with a certainty in my chest that I hadn't expected as I climbed in and closed the door behind me. It was the only thing that had felt right this whole weekend.

"Sure thing, miss. That's a real pretty apple you've got there," he said, nodding toward the piece of fruit I'd pulled out of my bag and bitten into. "Can't say I've seen one like that before."

An unwilling grin spread across my face. “No, you haven’t. They’re very unique,” I told him.

Just like the man who grows them.

Chapter 7

Lilith

Several weeks later

I POUNDED ON ALISTAIR'S door in a huff, even though I knew he wouldn't be awake yet. "Alistair! Get up! Your damn frog is back!"

I'd come home from work after *weeks* of frog-free living to find that silly frog back in my house. It's entirely possible that he'd been there longer than I realized because the pothos was getting a little unruly, but I glanced at the mushroom fae as I set down my purse and there he was, hiding in the leaves with them. *HOW DID HE DO IT?*

"It's unlocked," came a sleepy, muffled reply.

I pushed the door open and entered. "Why is your door unlocked?" I chastised him. "What if somebody—" I stopped in my tracks and promptly burst out laughing. "What are you *doing?*" I asked him incredulously.

He was lying face-down on his couch as though he were 'planking', his arms down by his sides, with his face literally pressed into the seat of the couch.

"Are you asleep?" I asked doubtfully as I leaned over to peer at him. "Is this how you sleep?"

He didn't reply other than to give an irritated buzz.

"You sleep like a baby owl?" I asked, cackling with delighted glee at the ridiculousness of it. I'd figured he probably didn't lie on his wings, but I had never imagined a full baby-owl-position.

He lifted his face off the couch seat to stare at me with bleary eyes. "What?" he asked, still sounding half asleep. *Oh, my heart.*

"Baby owls sleep sprawled out just like this, with their faces flat on the floor because their heads are too heavy for their bodies," I informed him, nearly in tears at the image before me. I couldn't stop laughing at the mental comparison. "Alistair, this is the cutest thing I've ever seen. Your antennae are a mess, by the way," I told him through my laughter.

He buzzed at me again and put his face back down, causing me to cackle even harder.

"No!" I squawked at him. "Get up! Your frog is back. Patrick! He's in my house again." I poked at his shoulder through the mounds of feathery gray fluff that covered it, surreptitiously enjoying the softness of it and the sparkly scales that came away on my fingers when I touched it.

Just the other day we'd sat together on this very couch, sipping mango smoothies and discussing our preferred medium for propagating plant cuttings—as I wondered privately what it would be like to kiss his face off—and I'd chuckled about how much glitter always fell out of his chunky-knit throw blanket.

"That one was a lost cause from the start, I'm afraid," he'd informed me. "I hand knitted it myself using that lovely homespun yarn the goblin who lives across the hall from you makes. You know Susan, right? Well, any fiber I touch is forever destined to be shiny. But it's so soft, isn't it?" The blanket was currently in a pile on the floor next to him.

Alistair made a grumpy noise at me and lifted his head again. "He's not *my* frog."

"You named him," I argued.

"I didn't name him! That's his name," he insisted. I was so used to Alistair's weirdness that it didn't even occur to me to ask how he knew the frog's name.

"He lives at your orchard," I protested, picking up his blanket and trying to drape the enormous thing across the back of his couch. "Why did you sleep on your couch? You're such a bachelor."

"I didn't expect little elves to come barging in before wake-up time," he mumbled into his seat, laughing when I made an outraged sound, and then wrapping his two left arms around me to pull me down onto the couch with him. "We need to find you some diurnal friends," he told me as he tucked me into his side. I was stunned, quietly delighting in the warm press of his body against mine and the deep, woodsy scent of him, so heavy I could drown in it. We were very comfortable with each other at this point, but that had never extended to *snuggling*.

I tried to act nonchalant, reaching to thread my fingers through his silky mane again and then smiling to myself when he gave a purring rumble. "All of my diurnal friends are back in New Caelora," I replied softly, thinking back to the loneliness I'd felt when I first moved here. *And then, when I went back, none of them had time to see me, except the one who wanted to use me after flaking out as my guest.*

"Do you miss them?" he asked sleepily.

I trailed a finger down one of the arms he had draped over me, marveling over the contrast of soft and hard, and how much strength and power it contained. "I did at first," I admitted. "Sometimes I still do." I did miss the occasional brunch or dinner date with my friends, but mostly, I missed having that network of people I knew had my back and that I could support too. Alistair was all I had here, and that didn't seem particularly healthy. Being reliant on him for every event or social need wouldn't work, even if I wanted it to.

"You don't have friends here?" he asked, making my stomach twist and my cheeks heat with embarrassment.

"Just you," I admitted with a shrug. I was slowly beginning to feel comfortable here, and he'd been enough for me, at least back when I'd been determined to get back home as soon as possible. The guy at the smoothie shop recognized me when I came in and always had my order ready to go without needing to be told what it was. I'd found a quaint little park near the nursery to visit on my lunch breaks that was becoming a comforting little ritual. There was an older lady who'd started coming into the plant nursery regularly to buy new flower bulbs. She was easy to talk with and always happy to see me, and I'd thought maybe she could be a friend some day, in an alternate universe where I stuck around in this weird little town. Although, friendships take time and effort, and I wasn't the most adept at that anyway. But I had found, since my trip home, that I wasn't chafing at being here so much, and I knew my fluffy, antennaed companion had more than a small part to play in that.

Alistair's arm tightened around me briefly in a tiny hug before turning his head to face me. I felt his hot breath against the top of my head. "You should meet my friends. They would like you."

I swallowed and aimed for a teasing tone. "Are they all nocturnal like you? Because that wouldn't help."

He huffed at me. "Only one of them. They meet up pretty regularly at a pub that Miela's dad manages in the Crown District. We could join them."

I gave a small shrug, feeling awkward about inserting myself further into Alistair's life, but knowing it would probably be good for me to meet some new people. “If you want to,” I finally said.

“I do,” he replied against the top of my head. I could hear the smile in his voice. “It’s a date, then.”

Chapter 8

Lilith

A SIGN HANGING OVER the entry named it The Silver Tongue, and fae lights flickered low in the windows as the sun began its slow descent early one evening.

We entered the cozy, modern-looking bar with dark, wood accents and industrial-style decor. Tables and seating were varied sizes for different species, a welcome sight that spoke of thoughtful management and a diverse neighborhood.

"Alistair! Come have a drink. We're celebrating!" A booming voice came from a burly-looking orc behind the bar as he skillfully poured a round of drinks for the customers clustered around the bar top. He towered over everyone except Alistair, who nearly matched him in height, but his hands moved nimbly among the glasses and bottles. His dark green skin was mottled with white patches that had themselves been decorated with some kind of runic tattoos. His slick black hair was pulled back into a tight topknot, and his green eyes peered through dark-rimmed glasses. The overall effect was a cacophony of beautiful monochrome color and texture on a dashing-looking orc.

"We are? What are we celebrating?" Alistair answered curiously as he led me by the hand to the bar top.

"I bought The Silver Tongue!" the big orc crowed, beaming as he raised his massive arms to indicate the bar around him. "I finally get to change the name to The Silver Tusk! Come on, introduce me to your friend." He leaned past the bar to give me a friendly wink, his silver capped tusks clearly visible over the curve of his smile. "What can I get for you, miss? First drink is on the house tonight!"

Congratulations from hollering patrons at the bar nearly drowned out the introductions, but I gathered that the bartender's name was Hyrak and one of the smiling girls seated at the bar top was Solandis, his wife, who also happened to be Alistair's oldest friend. She was sylvan—one of the forest fae—with long, white hair and pale, green skin, and the mother of Miela, the little toddler who'd caused such havoc at Alistair's orchard. She told me that despite their squabbling, Alistair was Miela's favorite babysitter, and she would live forever as a wild thing in his orchard if she were allowed. The sylvan's eyes danced with curiosity and interest as they darted back and forth between me and Alistair while she introduced herself.

"She'll have to stop eating all of my apples if she wants to take up permanent residence in my orchard," he replied amiably.

Next to Solandis was a tall, human-looking, blond woman with braided hair and fair skin named Sidney. "Oh! The one who bought him his workout shirts from the Void!" I remembered aloud.

The blond woman's smile was quick, and her eyes danced with mischief. "Aren't those great?"

Alistair explained that Solandis had grown up down the street from him, and they'd all attended college together. He introduced me to a few other regulars and explained their connections, and I was pleased with how deftly he directed the group's attention back to the normal flow of conversation so that I was no longer the focus. Solandis and Sidney kept me included, which I was grateful for, though they certainly took a somewhat sisterly interest in my relationship to Alistair. I was glad they didn't ask about specifics because I didn't know myself. He'd called tonight a date, but that was just a saying. It wasn't really, of course.

I began to relax as my margarita made its way into my veins, and I listened to the comforting low buzz of Alistair's voice as he spoke with his friends.

He turned down a third refill on his wine and requested a cider instead, which arrived frozen solid. "It's tradition," Hyrak had told him with a smirk, before finally giving in and getting him a new one when the mothman threatened to toss it at his head.

I didn't know how much alcohol it would take to affect someone of Alistair's stature, but I smiled to myself as I realized he was laughing more than usual. Was this Buzzed-Alistair? Or was it just because he was with his friends? It was a hilarious thought. And the way he interacted with his friends was amusing too. He was such a lovely mix of contradicting traits: shy, nervous, confident, flamboyant, smart, loyal, nurturing, persnickety, and gruff. He was always ready with a funny quip, and obviously a well-loved member of their circle of friends. Except maybe by Hyrak. It was hard to tell what the relationship was there. But even though he seemed to enjoy ruffling Alistair's feathers, the big orc couldn't seem to help but smile at some of my mothman's snark.

My mothman? Where had that thought come from?

Although, in retrospect it shouldn't have been such a surprise. I did sometimes wonder what that would look like, for him to be mine, but I'd never let myself go so far as to actually think of it as true. In that moment, daydreams quickly spun themselves one after another—me convincing Alistair to leave with me for New Caelora, introducing him to my best girlfriends and including him in our monthly girls' night out, showing him around to all of my favorite little bistros. But then I tried to picture him in my tiny, contemporary condo. After experiencing the loveliness of his old penthouse, that he had put so much time and careful thought into... the web of daydreams started to unravel a little bit. Where would he grow his beloved apple trees in my concrete and steel jungle?

The vibrations of his rumbling laugh jostled me out of my thoughts, and I tried to anchor myself in it, focusing on enjoying him for who he was right here. His body emanated a comfortable heat next to me, like he was an immense fuzzy blanket right out of the dryer. I found myself leaning closer than necessary whenever he spoke to me, seeking both his warmth and his presence. His feathery fluff was soft, like I would imagine a chinchilla or maybe mink fur to be, and the adorable sparkles he left on my skin every time he brushed against me smelled like comfort and happiness and desire in a way that didn't make sense to me. The shimmering patch of glitter that his gentle fingers left on my thigh every time he sought my attention in the overly loud bar felt like a brand. Like he'd marked me, and I enjoyed the idea a little too much.

I noticed that even though he kept an ear toward his friend's conversations, he had a careful eye trained on me as well. He checked in to make sure I was comfortable, asking if I was hungry or needed anything, quietly explaining the jokes someone cracked if I was missing context to understand them, whispering private observations about the more boisterous patrons across the bar as they teased and antagonized one another. It was the most fun I'd had with anyone in a very long time, and I settled into a happy contentment with him as the evening wore on.

"So, where is Miela this evening?" Sidney asked the orc and his wife when the bar began to quiet down, as she watched him shake me a new margarita.

"Oh, it's a grandma kind of night tonight," Solandis answered cheerfully, glancing over her shoulder as some of the louder customers finally left the bar. "They're baking special cookies and having a slumber party. Toenails will be painted. The whole works."

"Sounds adorable," Sidney responded as she crunched down on a pretzel.

"And who's with your baby?" Hyrak asked Sidney as he poured my drink and slid it in front of me. I cast him a grateful smile before redirecting my attention to the blond woman.

"A dragon is not a *baby*," she answered drolly. She shrugged and continued, "He's been more chill about hanging out on our property without me lately, as long as the pigeon stays with him, so they're at home together. Huck's been super cranky and hormonal lately, anyway. He either keeps himself wedged into the back of the cave behind our house and only comes out when

I bring him treats, or he's perched on top of our roof, trumpeting his territorial claim to the world. Jordan is convinced he's going to pull the whole house down on us any day now." She spoke like having a dragon with a pigeon friend on her roof was an everyday occurrence for her. As my wide eyes flitted between the rest of their friend group, everyone else nodded like this was expected.

"Poor guy," Hyrak replied as he wiped the countertop in front of her and paused to take a payment from another patron. "Puberty is the *worst*," he empathized.

Alistair shrugged and added in a thoughtful tone, "I have no memory of it."

Solandis slapped her hand on the bar top and nearly howled at him in indignation. "Of puberty? That's because you *checked out* for the entire process! Everyone *else* was suffering with mood swings and acne, dorking around with their best friends." She turned to address Sidney while gesturing accusingly at Alistair. "Not him! *My* best friend disappeared into a literal cocoon for *six months*. He left me all alone!" Her glower was fierce as Sidney gazed at Alistair with wide eyes.

Alistair gave them very little reaction as he slurped up the last drops of his cider with his long, tube-like tongue. "I would apologize, but I'm rather grateful that I wasn't aware of the metamorphosis process," he replied tartly, placing his empty glass into Hyrak's outstretched hand. His prissy tone tugged a smile to my lips.

"Wait, so did your whole body change like a butterfly?" Sidney interjected, staring into the middle-distance like she was trying to picture it.

"Yes!" Solandis answered for him emphatically, slapping her palm on the counter again as she spoke. Her words were a little slurred. "He went in looking like the chubby caterpillar I'd always known and loved and came out looking like a skinny version of this," she said, gesturing vaguely at Alistair's huge, winged form.

He pretended to be affronted by her description, recoiling slightly in mock-outrage. "I wasn't *chubby*. I needed extra fat stores to sustain me during the—"

"He had the most adorable baby chub. Rolls for days. I made him play dolls with me. He was my only real friend, and I missed him terribly. I was *abandoned*." A dainty frown eclipsed her pout as her eyes grew distant at the memory. She snapped out of it quickly and slurred, "But I will admit his fluff looks fabulous now that he's grown into it, and the wings are a pretty cool perk."

"And my antennae are very handsome," he added solemnly, lifting one of his upper arms to stroke the gossamer appendage.

"Very handsome," Solandis agreed with a nod before taking a sip of her drink.

"Stop it," Sidney groaned. "I know what you're doing."

"What am I doing?" Solandis asked in an innocent tone.

"You're getting Hyrak all riled up so he'll take you into the broom closet and bang your brains out. Again."

I nearly choked. I glanced at the big orc to find him glaring at Alistair with slightly luminescent green eyes, something I knew to be an orcish tell that his adrenaline levels were rising.

Solandis gasped loudly. "I would never—"

"You would and you do," Sidney stated flatly. "And you know what, it's almost dark, so maybe *I* want to use the broom closet this time," she added, glancing at her watch.

"Oh! Does that mean Jordan is coming tonight—" Solandis started, but Alistair cut her off.

"Is that why you only compliment my antennae when Hyrak is around?" he very nearly wailed.

I clasped one of his hands, reveling in the velvety softness of his fingers, and told the perturbed mothman, "I think you have beautiful antennae, Alistair." Oh, dear. I was definitely buzzed to have said that out loud.

"Gorgeous," Sidney added with a nod that also might have been slightly drunken. We were all tipsy.

"I do not!" Solandis argued. "I tell you how handsome and fluffy you are all the time, Al."

"I'm gonna jerk his antenna right out of his head," Hyrak grumbled as he thumped the glass he'd just polished onto the counter and removed his wife's half empty beer. He eyed Sidney's drink as well, but she closed her hands around it and gave him a look that dared him to take it.

"You keep your hands off my bestie," Solandis told the big orc. She turned to Alistair with a sly smile. "I only use you for your dashing good looks *sometimes*, Al."

A deep growl emanated from the bartender.

Alistair countered with an annoyed buzz as his antennae flattened back against his head.

"No!" He stood up, pointing at Solandis and then Hyrak. "No, you know what, *I'm* going to take the broom closet tonight. You *can't have it*." His tone was haughty as he lifted me from my seat with one arm. I cast a baffled but amused glance at Alistair's friends as he hauled me away, just in time to find my own startled confusion mirrored in their faces. It was only as I heard a door open that Sidney's cackling laughter pierced the silence. The door swung shut with a click, enveloping us in darkness, and Alistair set me down in front of him while he buzzed irritatedly.

I waited for him to regain his composure, trying and entirely failing to ignore how good he smelled this close—night air and warm musk, so rich I could reach out and touch it—eventually giving in and planting my face in the fluff on his chest and inhaling as deep as I could. Amazing. He was so big. Towering above me like a wall of heat. Soft. I wanted to bathe in his scent. I pressed my face against his sternum and tried to huff him, realizing I'd reacted to his scent whenever I was near him, and it was only getting stronger. "Why do you smell so good?" I asked him dreamily.

"Pheromones," he answered distractedly. "I confess I have no idea what the broom closet is for, other than the obvious."

"The obvious?" I repeated, feeling like the drinks were making me daft.

"For holding brooms," he answered dryly.

I snuffled a laugh into his fluff. "I believe they use it for sex," I explained with a giggle.

"*What?*" he squawked, causing me to recoil slightly at the pitch. "That is foul! I'm not going to have *sex* with you in a *broom closet*. There's a dirty mop *right here!*" Something clattered to my right, presumably the dirty mop.

"Oh," I responded through my giggles, as if that was a completely reasonable reaction. My brain locked onto the fact that he didn't object to sex with me, just with doing it in a broom closet. "Then what are we going to do?" I asked him.

He grew very still, and I held my breath, biting my lip as I waited for him to answer.

"What—what else—I mean to say, what else can we do?" his voice cracked as he stammered. The wall of him seemed to lean infinitesimally closer.

I grinned up at him in the darkness, feeling like a teenager again, with just enough tequila in my blood to make me bold. "You could kiss me," I suggested breathlessly. Poor Alistair was clearly out of his depth, but this was a predicament of his own making. He was the one who dragged me off to a broom closet like a caveman.

"But it's dirty in here—wait," he gasped. His whole body started to vibrate under my touch, and I felt all four of his hands close gently around my shoulders and upper arms, his talons barely grazing my skin. "You want to kiss me?" he squeaked. "Oh, no. Are you drunk?" His voice dropped, full of suspicion. I couldn't see a thing in the pitch black of the closet, but I could hear the frown in his voice. "You didn't have very much, but you are very small. Too small. What if —"

"I'm not drunk," I lied, cutting him off. I wasn't *drunk*-drunk. Tipsy at best. I was still in full possession of my faculties. He did smell *really good,* though. Maybe I was drunk on that. "Are you drunk?" I asked him, a plan forming in my head.

"Of course not!" He sounded offended. "Do you know how much alcohol it would take to make someone like me—"

I reached as high as I could in the darkness and grabbed him by the fluff, pulling him down by his neck and aiming for an approximation of where I thought his mouth would be with my own.

Chapter 9

Lilith

HE MET ME HALFWAY, and I only fumbled a little as I brushed my lips ever so gently against his. The excited buzz he gave in his chest made my heart hammer inside my own. The dense, soft, musky smell of him was thick in the air. It tickled the back of my brain and drove out all my self-consciousness as desire curled between my thighs. I kissed his soft bottom lip, nibbling and licking at it before moving to his top one, exploring his mouth with sensual presses that only left me wanting more. When I touched my tongue to the seam of his lips, he pulled back slightly, the frantic buzzing in his chest ending in an ascending chirp that nearly sounded like a question.

"*Oh...* Do that again," he breathed against my mouth before firmly taking control. He pressed me back against the wall, one hand gently tugging my chin higher as his tiny fangs nibbled at my lips. He had another hand in my hair, one tracing the column of my neck, and another trailing lazily across my collarbone. It was everything I could have dreamed of and more. And I had dreamed of it. A lot.

I moaned into his mouth and melted against his body, and he intensified his enthusiastic buzzing, his whole body vibrating with excitement, his fingers tightening briefly on my body. The low, swooping sensation in my pelvis made my breath hitch as I wondered what that vibration would feel like between my legs. Alistair's mouth was deliciously silky as he plied my lips before tentatively tapping at the tip of my tongue with his own. I'd always wondered what his tongue would feel like, and my nipples tightened at my new knowledge. Slippery, nimble, and hot. I sucked at it, eliciting a groan that sent a spark of heat up my spine.

He broke our kiss to catch his breath, as I stood weakly braced against the wall, the dense, shaggy fur of his mane pressing into my front repeatedly as he heaved for air. I released my grip on it and let my fingers trail down his massive shoulders to his chest, and finally to the fine, satiny velvet that covered the muscles of his abs. His vibrations turned into a purring rumble, and he pressed a chaste kiss to my cheekbone before dragging his lips down to my jawline and neck.

I arched to give him access and felt his sharp claws prick my scalp and neck. His tongue began its tapping exploration of my neck alongside the nibbles of his kisses. "Alistair," I gasped, as his tongue trailed back up my neck, "you have so many hands, and yet none of them are where I want them to be."

He paused in his exploration, giving me a nervous sounding click.

I released a breathless laugh. Of course he was nervous. I would have to be more explicit. Reaching for his hand in the dark, I grabbed the one on my shoulder and tugged it down to my breast.

He gave a happy sounding click that made me laugh in earnest and proceeded to wrap every one of his hands around each of my breasts and ass cheeks. He enthusiastically massaged, groped, plucked, and fondled while sucking at my neck. Faster than should have been possible, I was writhing against him, mindlessly seeking pressure with my hips.

Could he even…? I'd spent more time than I'd like to admit wondering how this mothman mated and what his plumbing looked like. Several races within the Boundlands had internal genitalia like he did, but I didn't know what it consisted of or how it worked. I felt my way down the bumps of his abs with my hands, pausing between his legs when I found a large bulge beneath his skin that hadn't been there previously.

He shifted against me, sucking harder on my neck, and I added more pressure as I rubbed at this new mound. *How to coax it out?* He released my breast and cupped my cheek, then responded as if he'd heard my thoughts. "Lilith. Darling. As much as that piece of my anatomy fervently wishes to make your acquaintance, I would prefer to do so somewhere a little more private. And sanitary."

I turned my head and nipped at his thumb, feeling restless and wound up. "That sounds good. Let's go somewhere more private. And sanitary." I still hadn't given up my exploration of this curious new development below his abdomen.

He gave a little shiver as my fingers discovered a depression in the middle of the mound, almost like a seam. "You want to—"

I cut him off. "Yes. Right now, even." My voice was husky. What I'd *meant* was that I wanted him to take me right here in the broom closet, because I was just babbling at this point and had forgotten the train of conversation. But he scooped me right up off the floor and tossed me over his shoulder like a caveman—Alistair, *my* Alistair, had *lost his mind*—and was out the closet door in an instant, his long legs eating up the ground. I heard him pick up my handbag as we passed the bar. "I must bid you farewell. We're leaving now," he said to his friends.

"What?" Solandis squawked through her outraged laughter. "You're just leaving us?"

"Goodbye!" he called back, even louder, not bothering to turn as he reached the door.

I knew my face was flushed, but I grinned and waved a little as he carried me out. They were nice girls.

"No one will ever be able to 'sneak off' to the broom closet ever again. Anyone who steps foot in there will come out shimmering like a disco ball," I heard Sidney say.

"What's disco?" Solandis asked before the door slammed shut behind us and the damp night air blanketed my skin.

"I know you're afraid of heights," Alistair started in a consoling tone, "but we would get home *much* faster if I flew us instead of taking transit. I also appear vaguely obscene in my current state—what with my genitalia trying to break free, such as it is."

I snickered and gave him permission to fly us home, warning him severely *not* to drop me. It was terrifying, and horrible, and entirely worth it, because within minutes we were in his bed. If I'd expected mounds of pillows and blankets, I would have been severely disappointed. The man had *one* pillow and *one* thick, whole cloth—and shimmery—quilt. I'd suspected as much after I found him sleeping face down like a plank. At least his headboard was a luxurious, tall, upholstered beige velvet. Which was perfect, because I hoped he was going to be slamming me into it shortly.

Alistair seemed a little shy again as he loomed over me, having had a chance to cool down on the flight over, but I wasn't going to allow for that. I stripped my shirt off, remembering the reaction he'd had to touching my breasts earlier, and then pulled him down for a kiss.

He kissed me once, twice, delving into my mouth each time, his claws trailing behind my ear and down my neck, and we were right where we had left off. His buzzy purr as he nuzzled and kissed my neck made my face split into a wide grin, but the groan when I stroked my fingers down his chest and abs made me crazy. Alistair was a boob guy. Taking my shirt off had been the right call. He quickly worked his way down and then spent the next eternity kissing and sucking each one in turn, working me into a frenzy. I was panting and sweating, aroused to the point of painfulness by the time he peeled my pants off. I think he probably had several bald patches in his coat from where I'd gripped him too tightly, but he didn't seem to mind.

"I'm on birth contr—*oh!*" I choked out as his tongue darted out and licked a long, hot line up my slit. "Oh, stars. Give a girl some warning next time," I gasped as he suctioned onto my clit, his own grin making an appearance as he knelt between my legs.

He chuckled as he leaned in closer to my apex. "Like this, you mean?" His mouth pressed against my opening, lips rubbing and kissing, teasing and light. I spread my legs wider, inviting more of his attentions, and pressed my head back against the pillow, trying to be patient but needing more pressure. "Mm, that's a pretty sight," his voice buzzed against my clit, making my eyes roll back.

I forced my eyes open again to see my breasts thrust into the air as I arched my back, just as his velvety soft hands closed over them.

"I've wanted this so much," he breathed against me.

"You have?" I asked in wonder.

"Every day," he agreed. "For weeks and weeks."

"Why didn't you tell me?" I wanted to yell. But I knew. It was the same reason I hadn't told him.

We were shy.

I wasn't planning on staying.

We didn't know if our affections would be returned... We were so ridiculous.

His tongue was sending pleasurable tingles racing up my spine when I felt his antennae brush my sides, skimming up across my breasts to my neck and collarbone and back again. They were wispy and ticklish, the feathery filaments reminding me of ostrich plumes.

"What are you doing?" I giggled, twitching as he found a particularly ticklish spot, only for him to pin my hips down as he continued to lick me.

"Enjoying your scent."

"With your *antennae?*" I laughed.

"Our antennae are a highly adapted olfactory organ. I can smell you for miles," he said matter-of-factly.

That was a shocking statement, but I couldn't hold on to it, because I was desperately trying to keep from snapping my legs closed around his head. I didn't have anything resembling that skinny-girl thigh-gap, and he was probably in actual danger of suffocating. I didn't want to murder Alistair in the throes of lust. His feathery ruff was brushing against my inner thighs and the backs of my legs, his feathery antennae brushing against my breasts and abdomen. He had two hands on my breasts, plucking gently at nipples and massaging, two rubbing my ass, and he began working his long tongue inside of me as he sucked on my clit. My heart was thrumming a mile a minute as he started buzzing and humming and thrusting his long tongue. I came so forcefully I tried to fold in half, but he held me down.

The giant mothman sat back on his haunches, a huge grin on his face as I lay bonelessly sprawled in front of him. But that grin wasn't what had my focus. Between his thighs, a giant cock the likes of which I'd *never* seen stood thick and proud. My mouth dropped open.

"Wow, Alistair. Uh—"

His cock was—I hoped—fully distended from the area where the bulge I'd felt previously was located. It was longer than my forearm, impossibly thick, and pearly pink on the shaft with a tapered, crimson head that thrust out of a large fold at the end. More fat, heavy folds and veins decorated the length of it, and the whole thing twitched slightly with his heartbeat. The skin looked slippery with some kind of self-lubricant, and pre-cum already leaked from the tip.

"Oh!" He told me in a cheerful, confident tone as I sat up to inspect it. "This is my shuttle!" He palmed his cock in one of his many hands. "It's very similar to the genitals of your males, except that it's stored inside my body," he gestured to his lower abdomen, "until I am sufficiently aroused enough to force it out."

"And this?" I asked, pointing at the firm, bulbous band that bulged out around the base of his cock.

"That's my knot," he explained brightly before dropping into a more comfortable, educational tone. "It's called a vesica. It swells with sexual arousal and holds my shuttle"—he gestured proudly to his cock—"outside of my body for breeding. Then it swells even further during copulation to lock me inside a female's receiving orifice."

Receiving orifice. I mouthed the words. *This guy*. Wait, his cock would lock us together? "How long would it lock us together?" I asked warily, not having any experience with such a thing. I reached out to palm his cock as I asked, wanting to familiarize myself with it. The folds on it were dense but spongy, and the shaft was firm but had a little bit of give. It was hard to say because I couldn't wrap one hand around it—my fingers just barely overlapped if I wrapped two hands around it—but I thought with the outer sponginess that maybe we could make it work.

His teeth clacked shut as I rubbed at it. "Oh, that's... that's lovely. That feels... Oh." His breath shuddered out of him, and then he gritted his teeth as he swallowed convulsively, before finally remembering my question. "It isn't terribly long, I think. Perhaps five to ten minutes? We don't have to do that. I'd be terribly afraid of harming you."

I firmed my grip around him and let the skin slide through with the aid of his lubricant. His antennae twitched wildly. "Because you're so big?" I asked innocently.

"You are very small," he breathed out raggedly.

I bit my lower lip as I considered that, watching his face as I stroked him. He looked like he was in agony, and it was delightful. I wanted more of that. "I think I'd like to try," I told him, crowding his lap so that I could rub the tip of his cock along my opening.

"Oh, goodness," he wheezed as I lined him up and eased down on the tip. His whole body was vibrating with anticipation. I focused on taking him a little at a time, stretching myself around his girth, thankful for the lubrication that flowed out of me from his earlier efforts, as well as the slick coating he provided himself. Every bump and fold promised this would be a worthwhile endeavor, if I could just get him inside me. We were both panting heavily by the time I had him fully hilted, except for his knot. I didn't think that would make it inside. I felt impossibly full, stretched to the max, and when I clenched around his cock, all the breath gusted out of him.

He'd been a perfect gentleman, waiting patiently no matter how much it pained him while I worked my way down onto his shaft, his fingers all clenched into the bed underneath him. But now he groaned and rolled his hips, and then, panting and deciding that wasn't enough, rolled me onto my back and pushed back into me. He was vibrating intensely, and I knew he was trying not to thrust because he didn't want to hurt me.

I gripped his ass, the one I'd stared at so many times in our yoga classes, and told him he could move.

He pulled out slowly before thrusting back in until I could swear I could see the tip of his cock bulging against my belly, rolling his hips until he was fully sheathed inside of me, and then repeating the process. "Lilith," he said in a rumbling rasp. "This is... I fear that breeding you has become my new favorite thing."

I couldn't respond. I was in another dimension. I hadn't known that it was possible to have my consciousness dicked out of me, but that's exactly what he was doing. His size when he was pressed over me like this was overwhelming, his shaggy mane and muscular arms and chest like a hot, silky wall against my body. His hands stroked the sides of my abdomen and breasts before reaching his lower two down to grip my thighs. I was grateful for our yoga classes as he pulled my knees up to my ears so he could bury more of his cock inside me, finally breaching my opening with his knot. I could feel the intense *pop* every time he thrust it inside of me. His wings began to pulse behind him, powering his momentum as he picked my lower half up off the bed with the force of each of his thrusts. His enthusiastic vibrations pushed me over the edge. I orgasmed three more times before he finally plunged into me, his knot swelling far larger than I had expected, and emptied his hot seed inside my body. We lay there gasping for several minutes, locked together at our point of contact, and enjoyed our sweaty, enforced cuddle time.

"My plants will all die," he mumbled tiredly.

"What? Why?" I laughed at the strange non sequitur.

"Because this is all I want to do for the rest of my life."

Chapter 10

Lilith

THE NEXT FEW DAYS were a blur of not-enough-sleep for both of us and more "enforced cuddle time" than was probably healthy. It became a game to see how quickly I could force Alistair's "shuttle" from its hiding place within his body, and my questing fingers and bare breasts were often enough to leave him a babbling, twitchy mess with a drooling cock. We ravished each other nearly every moment we weren't at work, and it was painfully difficult to tear myself away from his vibrating, thrusting body long enough to eat. I spent more time at his place than my own, making sure to stop in to check on my plant and weird little toadstools, but otherwise we were working or in his apartment. He'd even started tucking me into his bed at night, complete with a kiss on the forehead, before he left for work.

I refused to think about the future, living in complete denial that anything could ever change. I was simply content to be amazed that he felt the same way about me that I did about him.

One evening I came home from work early, and since I knew he wouldn't be awake yet—and I wouldn't be able to keep my hands off of him if I were close enough to touch him—I stopped by my apartment downstairs to check on the mushrooms and make me some tea. It would give me a distraction so he could sleep longer without me pawing at him with my greedy little hands.

I'd just filled my kettle and set it on the stove when a spectral messenger glimmered into existence above the worktop to my left. I blinked at the unexpected flicker of light, taking a moment to comprehend that I needed to pay the toll, and then reaching into my pocket to take hold of the little calling stone that was hidden there and push a tiny bit of my magic into it.

"Good eve, my lovely Lilith." Boylen's voice drifted from the swirl of light, taking me by surprise.

It was all at once comforting and concerning. The timbre of his voice reminded me of my childhood—of potting up seedlings with my mother in the back room of her brother's nursery, of filching candies from the bowl in his office that I figured out later he only ever put out when he knew I'd be coming, of helping unload supply deliveries for him as a teen for overly generous amounts of pocket money, of pep talks and consoling pats when an interaction with a customer didn't go the way I wanted after he'd officially hired me, of an offer to take over his position as the day-to-day manager at his beloved nursery. But I was also concerned because there was something off in his voice. A tiredness that wasn't usually there, or apprehension perhaps.

"Good eve, Uncle Boylen," I greeted in return, allowing the spectral time to convey my message. "Is something wrong?"

A dry chuckle sounded into the empty space, followed by a barely audible sigh. "You know me too well, Lilith. No, no, nothing is *wrong*, as it were. I've just had a lot on my mind today. I'm calling because we need to discuss the *other* niece in my employ."

"Melantha? What's wrong with Melantha?" The kettle began to hiss, so I removed it from the heat and poured it into the teapot to steep.

"It appears it is time to do some restructuring."

Confusion set in, various scenarios flipping through my mind, and I paused in my pouring, holding the kettle aloft while I thought. Surely he would have told me if she'd been failing at her job or he needed to replace her as a manager for one reason or another.

He continued, unable to see my obvious bewilderment. "Her husband is nearly finished with his internship at the clinic here in the city, and as expected, was offered a permanent position there."

"Oh, that's great!" Relief flooded me. I was happy for her and her husband, Ellin. She'd told me often how hard he'd worked to secure that internship and the full-time employment that he hoped it would bring at the kinesthetics clinic for wyverns. He loved working with the smaller ones the cart drivers used and had even taken an interest in the racing wyverns at the local track.

"It is," my uncle agreed. "However, he's *also* been offered a position a few hours away at the clinic in Eastwood Heights."

"*Oh.*" I suddenly saw the problem. If he took the position in Eastwood Heights, the commute would be too far for Melantha to work at Blossom and Bonsai any longer, and my uncle suddenly had a management opening to fill there… or at my shop, if he needed me to come back and take my old position already.

"Indeed," he agreed, hearing all my unspoken conclusions from that one syllable. "And after much discussion, they've decided to leave their decision up to you."

"To me?" I repeated, utterly baffled. What did I have to do with it?

"Well, yes, to decide what you want to do. The management position here at Blossom and Bonsai is still yours, as I said it was when you left. And if you do plan to come back to it, then it would make the most sense for Melantha and Ellin to go ahead and relocate for this job offer."

"I didn't know not coming back to it was an option." I heard myself say the words, but I hadn't meant to speak them. I shook my head at myself and finished emptying the kettle into the teapot as he replied.

"Why wouldn't it be an option? You make me sound like some kind of slave driver," he said with a confused laugh. But my statement hadn't entirely been about him. I'd just never personally considered *not returning* as an option. It had been my entire goal ever since he'd brought up purchasing this second nursery. Hadn't it? My mind flickered to Alistair. I wasn't ready to leave yet.

"Melantha is happy enough in your position here as head manager, and as you saw on your recent visit, she has nearly—*not quite*, mind you, but nearly—grown into the shoes you left for her to fill. She's not there yet, but she will be. But of course, the position still belongs to you and is yours to return to, if you want it. The question is: *do you want it?* Because if you do plan to return to it, then they need to know that so they can make plans to relocate to Eastwood Heights soon so he can take the position there. However, if that is the case, then I would need you to return in the next week or so to take over for her here so that they can begin relocating. Stars know I'm too old for the daily task of management anymore, but I could do it for a week or two if I must." I ignored his grumbling. The man was barely over 100 years old, which was hardly old at all for an elf.

"What would happen here?" I asked numbly. "What about The Floral Dilemma?"

"We could sell it," he said, and even as he said it, I rejected the notion. "You've done such a nice job revitalizing it that I could easily turn a tidy profit already."

"I don't want to sell it." It wasn't mine to sell, but I knew my uncle would respect my wishes anyway.

"Well, it's running well enough that if you think your man Artem could handle it, you could appoint him to management," he offered, sounding unsure. He knew from their brief interactions just as well as I did how little Artem liked interacting with customers. "Or hire another manager. Or," he continued, "if you are content to continue on as you are at The Floral Dilemma, then I could grant her this position permanently and her husband would take the position at the clinic here. She said both clinics have positives and negatives and he's open to both placements. But then you would no longer have the option to return here as manager, so that's why we all thought it would be best for you to choose what you wanted to do, and then Melantha and Ellin will make their plans from there. I hate to put you on the spot, my dear Lilith, but he will need to respond to these job offers shortly."

I wanted to tell him I would return. *Of course I would return.* I'd done what I'd set out to do—I'd remade the shop, made it profitable, and was working on creating a steady enough flow of customers to make it sustainable. I'd pretty much completed all my goals. Mostly.

I ignored the pang of discomfort I felt about leaving behind The Floral Dilemma. It's not like I was attached to the little store or the new regulars who'd started to pop in on delivery days to see what new plants were available. Or the grumpy old dryad. Or the peppy, chipper dwarf who drove us crazy. I just didn't like leaving things unfinished, that was all. Artem wouldn't be *happy* about being left in charge, but he was more than capable, in my opinion. And surely he wouldn't turn his nose up at whatever raise Boylen would ply him with for taking on the extra duties.

Alistair was a harder pang to ignore. The thought of not getting to see him again didn't feel good at all. *At all.*

"Can I have a little bit of time to think about it?" My voice was shakier than I expected it to be, and Boylen's tone took on a gentler inflection.

"Of course, dear one. And listen, I don't want you to worry about me. You've spent your whole life working to make me proud, and you have. I am so proud. I've loved having the chance to work so closely with my family, and I adore you and Melantha both. You're both good, strong workers, and I couldn't ask for better. There is no wrong answer here for either of you. I want you to do what makes you happy."

I was near tears as I thanked him and released the messenger, leaving my pot of tea untouched on the counter. I found myself drifting into the living room, standing in front of the pretty little pothos that Alistair had gifted me and actively ignoring the presumably judgy stares of the mushrooms and the warty little frog that had forcibly inserted themselves into my home and my heart. Alistair's advice had been to simply allow the frog to stay and make sure he had a dish of water and feed him grubs. *Grubs!*

Well, if they insisted on being here, they could bear witness to my existential crises.

"How am I supposed to sort this out?" I asked the potted menagerie. Patrick simply blinked his big, empty eyes at me. No thoughts. The toadstools pretended like they couldn't hear me.

I knew what my heart wanted.

But I also knew what was smart. Safe. Routine. Normal. I had my condo, and my friends, my family, all my familiar creature comforts back in New Caelora. The thought of shutting the door on all of that and starting a new life here was hard. *I liked my old life*. My mind drifted back to the wedding, though, to how unhappy I'd been the whole time I'd been home and how desperately I'd just wanted to come back to Alistair, and we hadn't even been together at that point.

Strangely, Alistair's words from a conversation directly before that weekend came back to me then, from when he'd introduced me to the fuzz berry pastries and was describing how he missed the delicate fruit. *"But, I think, somehow, that fleeting window of availability, their rarity, their uniqueness... It all makes them that much more special."* His words weighed heavy on my heart.

My window of availability for what I really wanted was fleeting, and unlike the fruit, I wasn't willing to bank on this one coming around again.

I decided I wasn't going to miss it.

Chapter 11

Alistair

A LIGHT TAP SOUNDED at my door, which was odd, because I knew from her scent that it was Lilith and we were well beyond the 'polite knocking' stage. So it was with an uneasy feeling that I opened the door.

She stood on the other side, holding my favorite little Ice Princess pothos, which I'd gifted to her so she could rehome the low-fae that had taken up residence in her house. Patrick the frog sat nestled under one of the leaves with his ever-placid expression betrayed by the rapid flickering of his tiny throat pouch as he hyperventilated. The toadstool-fae—*nympha mordens*—were doing their very best to appear as real mushrooms, nervously tilting their tiny faces downward to be less visible. They despised being transported.

"Is something wrong?" I asked, discomfort spiking as we made eye contact and I found that hers were troubled. Did she not want my plant any longer? Perhaps she wanted her tree back in exchange. I would happily give it back, but the pothos had been a gift. We didn't need to make an exchange. Or maybe Patrick had stopped eating the grubs I'd recommended for his feeding, and carrying the little pot was preferable to touching the frog. That I could understand—being opposed to the feeling of the mucus-like secretions myself—but I would have come down to her apartment to observe him if she'd asked.

I took a moment to drink in her features, noting the disquiet written across them. Her perfect, delectable lips were turned down at the corners. Her adorable, expressive eyebrows were currently pinched above the freckles that scattered across her pert, elvish nose. Her silken chestnut hair that just brushed her delicate jawline, clenched with tension. The radiant-looking skin that was paler than usual. Her beautifully rounded cheeks and soft figure that felt so perfect wrapped in my arms. I wanted to pull her into my arms right now, but she was holding herself strangely distant.

Her voice was emotionless when she finally spoke. "My uncle says the new nursery is doing well enough that he could trust someone else to run it now, and he has my place at the old store waiting for me if I want it."

She was leaving.

I'd known this was coming. She'd talked about her old city regularly for as long as I'd known her. She'd made it clear that she wasn't staying here long term. I'd known it, but I hadn't believed it. I'd hoped I'd have longer to woo her, had been in denial that this day would ever actually come. Hearing her speak the words felt like a blow to the chest.

"Oh," I said, my voice cracking despite my attempt to control my emotions. "Well, that's... that's great. Right?" I made myself say the words, easily hearing the lie in them anyway. "That's what you wanted, isn't it?"

I forced a smile even though it felt terrible. I didn't feel like smiling. I felt like my heart was splintering into a million pieces. My sternum must have been splitting in two. My chest cavity was breaking open, ready to spill my internal contents all over the floor at her feet. I had been happily going about my life with it revolving around my work and my research, my beloved apple trees easily existing as the center of my universe. Solandis would occasionally drag me out for a night with our mutual friends or I'd spend a day with her daughter, whom I adored. Sometimes I played cards with Sidney's vampire husband and his nocturnal co-workers. My life was fine. Until Lilith plunged into it with her alluring scent and her bright smiles, more illuminating than any lamplight. How would I attend our yoga classes without her sunny laughter as she fumbled a pose and collapsed on her mat? How would I come home in the morning and not have her comforting scent drifting up through the registers? How would I go on without her compassion and her stories, her intelligence and her wit? Without her whimpers and moans as she took me inside her body?

I couldn't.

My life stretched out before me, dim and drab and lonely and entirely unappealing. But I forced a smile, because it's what she wanted.

My alarm spiked higher as her face crumpled distressingly and she burst into tears, clutching her plant pot to her chest more tightly in my doorway.

"I don't think it is," she cried, and my heart hammered in my chest.

"What? What—what?" I stammered. My eyes were wide as I reached for her automatically, pulling her into my apartment and shutting the door behind her, taking her pot in one hand and guiding her to my couch with another. I sat down with the little pot on my lap and pulled her into the seat next to me, wrapping several arms around her and holding her against my side. "Talk to me," I soothed, my mind racing.

"I don't want to go home," she sobbed, her tears leaking into my mane. I should have been disturbed, but I wasn't. Her bodily fluids never bothered me the way everything else did.

"What's wrong?" I asked. This was what she wanted. I knew it was.

"I hated this town. Hated it here. But I didn't know anyone! Nothing was the same, and I felt so alone. All I could think about was biding my time until I could go back to my old life. But I don't want to leave you."

I nodded and held her closer. I didn't want her to leave me either, but I couldn't make this harder for her. Letting her talk through her feelings was the best thing I could do right now.

"I don't want to leave this," she sniffled, scrubbing under her eyes. "What do you want?" she asked, her gaze sharpening on mine.

I swallowed thickly, trying to decide how to answer. "I want you to be happy," I said slowly, willing it to be true. I did want her to be happy, but not really, not if it meant her leaving.

"Do you want me to move home?" she asked bluntly.

"No." My answer was automatic, the tiny word out in the open before my brain could even process that I'd spoken. But once it was, the floodgates were broken. "No. I want you to stay here and move in with me. I don't ever want to be without you. I don't want you to move home. I... I want this to be your home."

Silence reigned as she took in my answer. She chewed on her lip for long enough that I feared she might damage it, and I reached up to tug it gently from her teeth. Lilith blew out a heavy breath and then nodded. "I need you to take care of my plant."

I stared at her, unable to piece together what she was saying.

"While I go home and get my condo ready to sell," she clarified. "Will you be capable of feeding those grubs to Patrick? I know you hate bugs," she said with a hiccup from too many tears.

I carefully set the pot on the floor and then tackled Lilith onto the couch, pinning her beneath me as I kissed her over and over again. I would feed Patrick a thousand horrible bugs for this woman. She was going to *live* with me.

Epilogue

Alistair

"WHAT ARE WE GOING to do with Patrick while Miela is here on Saturday?"

"I could always take him back to the orchard," I offer. He won't be able to get back inside my apartment—I actually bother to lock my windows, unlike Lilith. Patrick is living here of my own goodwill, and because I think—secretly—he makes my darling happy. She might huff and puff about him getting into her apartment repeatedly, but that's just because she never caught on to the fact that the toadstools were the ones doing it. I think she considers him some kind of strange pet now.

"No, that's okay," she says quickly, confirming my suspicions, and glances past me toward my bedroom. *Our* bedroom. "We can just move the pot into the bedroom and shut the door while she's here, to spare him from more toddler harassment." Miela's aggressive affection for unsuspecting wildlife is genetically coded into her very being, as far as I can tell. She's a potent mix of her mother's sylvan affinity for small living things, as well as her mischievousness and sass, with a solid dose of her father's orcish tenacity and temper. She couldn't be more perfect.

"What time is Hyrak bringing her?" Lilith asks.

"Before his shift starts at noon," I tell her as I unpack her drink from the sack I'm holding. "I just told the barista to make you your regular."

"Oh, thank you! Hey, what's the deal with you and Hyrak, anyway? Things seemed a little tense that one night at the bar. Is he jealous of your friendship with Solandis?"

"He is an orc," I answer with a shrug. Orcs are well known for their ferocious jealousy of their mates. Hyrak isn't a full-blooded orc, and thankfully, his instincts seem to fall on the milder side. I've known some rather bestial orcs, but I have to admit his frontal cortex is a little more developed than usual. "Don't worry," I assure her. "We have an understanding."

"What's that?" she asks, taking a sip of her smoothie. "Oh, that's delicious. He made it perfectly," she murmurs, her pleasure over even this small thing thrilling me to my core. "Do you mean, like, that you're Solandis's best friend and Hyrak is her lover and you should support each other? That's really mature—"

"Oh." I shake my head and scoff. "No. Mostly that he could crush my exoskeleton with his bare hands and I could drop him from a very great height," I explain blithely with a wave of one of my hands. "Also, he likes my apples."

She barks a laugh, muttering something under her breath that sounds like, "Men are dumb," but she's smiling as she says it.

I ignore her comment and pull out a chair to take a seat at the table next to the light of my life, dragging my knitting toward me so I have something to do with my hands while we chat. Lilith has asked for her own version of my hand-made chunky-knit blanket, and I am happy to oblige. I can knit them in half the time by knitting them in two panels, one with each set of hands, then stitching them together.

"Speaking of your apples," she starts, and I glance up at her from my project, "I was thinking about adding a little refreshments area, like a little bistro, at the nursery. I could use your amazing Moon Blush to make some custom hand-pressed juice blends, like apple and pomegranate, or apple and mango."

My horrified gasp causes her to whip her head up. "That's atrocious! You would sully my precious Moon Blush with something as inferior as pomegranate?" What would be next? *Actual garbage?*

She rolls her eyes and swats at me with the sack from her drink. "You dork. Help me find an apple press."

"Fine." This right here is proof of my love for her. "Actually, I think I might have a good source of pomegranates for you," I admit with a smile. I might not like them as much as apples, but I like that she is looking toward the future and thinking about building her life here. *With me.*

*

Want more of the Boundlands crew? Keep reading for more stories set in this world!

Green-Eyed Monster

He's an orc studying for his accounting exam. She's a forest faerie trying to salvage her botany project. There's a magically animated stone sentry crashing through campus like a two-story tall wrecking ball.

The first time Hyrak lays eyes on Solandis, he's too immersed in the chaos around them to notice her soft beauty, but once she's in his arms, he's enchanted by the opinionated little fae's passion. Can gentle Hyrak control the fiery possession scorching through his veins? Does Solandis really want him to?

GREEN-EYED MONSTER is a short (10K word), fun monster romance with a guaranteed HEA. Content warnings include adult language and consenting adult romantic scenes.

Get a free copy when you sign up for my newsletter at elsiewinters.com!

Leviathan's Song

When Elara races to save a dying city, her best hope lies with a seductive siren… but brooding Levi has his own reasons for keeping her at arm's length.

As an elven weapon smith, Elara is an expert in crafting beautiful, deadly things. When an underwater city known as the Deep sends for her help, she's determined to answer the call… but between murderous gangsters and razor-sharp foreign politics, Elara is ill-equipped to handle the situation on her own.

Levi Navarre is half-merman and all brooding, sardonic wit. Landlocked, jaded, and rejected by his people, the last thing Levi wants to do is get involved in underwater affairs. But soft-hearted, strong-willed Elara is a temptation he just can't resist... even if she is several miles out of his league. Levi has good reason to avoid the obvious magical bond forming between him and Elara—but if he isn't careful, playing bodyguard could soon turn into something more...

Available Now

Magpies & Mayhem

What happens when you stumble upon your childhood crush, only to discover that he's been turned into a vampire?

I feel like I spend my whole life putting out fires. That's probably just part of the territory with being a magpie-shifter from such a chaotic family. All I want is to keep my loved ones safe and have some fun. I've never been cut out to be the responsible one.

And Jordan Houjin is still everything I remember ... hot, sexy arrogance and smoldering smart mouth. Except now he's angry at the world and disappears every time I run into him. But that's fine because I want nothing to do with a vampire my family would never accept anyway. Don't I?

Unfortunately, he's the only one I know who can help me keep this dragon egg alive.

Available Now

Seduction of a Psychopomp

Erogenous Hand Holding and Other Ways to Tame Your Reaper

I won't live to see my 29th birthday unless I make a deal to marry Death.

An arranged marriage to a grim reaper? Whatever keeps me on this side of the dirt.

My new husband Victor is formidable, built like a god, and ... is scary supposed to be this sexy? Because it's kind of sexy. The problem is he doesn't seem to *get* this whole marriage thing. Every time I approach him for company, he scampers off like a disgruntled cat. I'd be fine with letting him have his space, but I can't help being reminded every time I look at him that a girl has *needs*. How can I lure my new husband into bed? And is it even possible to win the heart of a reaper?

Available Now

Acknowledgements

My books are never a one-woman effort and I'm incredibly grateful for everyone who helps me finish them. A special thanks to Susan R, SL Prater, Erin Vere, Colleen Crowley, Lisette Marshall, Vela Roth, and CM Nascosta for all of their time, effort, advice, and emotional support as I write. Thank you to each of you who reads, reviews, and shares my books.

Thank you to Amira Naval, who painted my gorgeous cover and didn't flinch when I asked for a mothman, and to Leigha Wolffe-Stoirm, who edits my manuscripts and hides as many of my grammar sins as I will allow. Any mistakes found within are my own, because she probably flagged it and I ignored it. You two are some of the best teammates and friends a girl could ask for and I acknowledge and appreciate how much of my nonsense you put up with.

Thank you to all of you for making this job *fun*.

Also By Elsie Winters

Green-Eyed Monster

Leviathan's Song

Magpies & Mayhem

Seduction of a Psychopomp

Live, Laugh, Lurk

About the Author

Elsie Winters writes sweet, cozy comfort reads with a dash of spice and a dollop of fantasy. Her favorite pastimes are feeding the birds who knock on her window for snackies and spending way too much money on plants. She also reads paranormal romance books like they're going out of style and collects monster art that she has to hide from her kids.

Never miss a story! Check out my website to sign up for my newsletter or follow me on social media!

Contact info:
www.elsiewinters.com
elsie@elsiewinters.com

www.ingramcontent.com/pod-product-compliance
Lightning Source LLC
Chambersburg PA
CBHW030939210726
48290CB00007B/2258

* 9 7 8 1 7 3 7 5 3 5 5 6 0 *